DISSEVERED

Translated from the Bengali original

Khandita

by

Rani Ray

SAMARESH BOSE

THORNBIRD

NIYOGI BOOKS

Published by
NIYOGI BOOKS
Block D, Building No. 77,
Okhla Industrial Area, Phase-I,
New Delhi-110 020, INDIA
Tel: 91-11-26816301, 26818960
Email: niyogibooks@gmail.com
Website: www.niyogibooksindia.com

Design: Nabanita Das

ISBN: 978-93-89136-06-7
Publication: 2019

This is a work of fiction. The names, characters and incidents portrayed in it are the work of the author's imagination. Any resemblance to actual persons, living or dead, events or localities, is entirely coincidental.

Printed at: Niyogi Offset Pvt. Ltd., New Delhi, India

Introduction

The English translation of Samaresh Bose's Bengali novel *Khandita* (meaning 'cleft into two', written in 1985) comes out at a time when we have already completed seventy years of independence. The birth pangs of independence are described by him through the eyes of three young Bengali friends who experienced the midwifery of partition that tore apart our subcontinent in 1947. The English version of Samaresh's novel will find echoes among the survivors of that partition-cum-independence period, and their descendants who are living across the borders in India, Bangladesh, and Pakistan—who must have gone through similar experiences as the characters of this novel. It also opens up to the post-independence generation of readers, a moment of history, when our people were caught up in a peculiar amalgam of ecstasy (at the thought of independence from British rule), sadness, and apprehensions (caused by the territorial partition that uprooted thousands from their homeland)—and yet, a lingering hope (that the two amputated hands of Bengal would hold each other one day).

This novel can be termed as 'documentary fiction'—a literary genre which uses authentic historical material, and usually incorporates it verbatim in its narrative, but presents it through the techniques and forms of fiction. It is in the tradition of Tolstoy's historical novel *War and Peace*, Jean Paul Sartre's trilogy *Roads to Freedom* (set in France around the time of World War II), and Illya Ehrenburg's *Fall of Paris*, which records the decay and collapse of French society between 1935 and the German occupation in 1940. In a similar style, Samaresh Bose weaves documentary reports into fiction, while narrating the experiences of his characters during a crucial period in our history. As an eyewitness to the events of those days of 1946–47, Samaresh covers a wide historical and cultural gamut, making the readers relive those events through his vivid description of the numerous facets of contemporary Bengali society—debates between Congressmen and communists in politics, literary experiments in the middle-class milieu, working-class grievances in the industrial suburbs of Calcutta, as well as the exploitation of folk artistes in the post-partition era.

The events and political personalities described in the novel constituted an important part of the twin story of partition and independence in Bengal. Gandhi opposed partition, and when the murderous communal riots broke out on the eve of independence in 1947, he alone undertook a journey of peace to Noakhali in East Bengal (now a part of Bangladesh), and later on in the riot-torn Beliaghata area of Calcutta, where he went on a fast to end the riots. Among the other personalities mentioned in the story is Huseyn Shaheed Suhrawardy, the controversial Muslim League Chief Minister of Bengal at that time. According to contemporary accounts and rumours, he was accused of sponsoring the deadly communal riots in Calcutta in 1946 (an allegation that figures in the conversations among the characters in this novel). But official documents (released now) have exonerated Suhrawardy, by disclosing the record of his attempts to quell the riots (Re: 'Suhrawardy no Nero, show Bengal files', by Shiv Sahay Singh in *The Hindu*, September 30, 2015). In fact, he stayed with Gandhi in Beliaghata to help him halt the communal strife (Re: Sumit Sarkar: *Modern India: 1885–1947*; p. 438, Macmillan India Ltd., 1983). On the eve of partition, he aligned with the Bengali Congress leader Sarat Bose in a campaign for a separate state of a 'United Bengal' (instead of its partition between Pakistan and Indian Union). When that failed, after partition, he migrated to East Pakistan and continued to play an important role in the political scene there.

The train journey of the three friends from their hometown, which initially began from their desire to meet Gandhi in Calcutta, takes a different turn when they seek to have 'just a glimpse of a new country, to see how new it looks' (meaning East Pakistan, the newly separated part of Bengal). During the journey to East Pakistan, their encounter with the elderly Syed Badruddin in their train compartment reveals to them the other fraternal dimension of Bengali Hindu–Muslim relations at that time (as opposed to the mutually hostile communal dimension that led to the partition). Through Badruddin's didactic discourse, and his open invitation to the three Hindu Bengalis to be his guests, Samaresh seeks to address two major issues in Bengal in the late 1940s—(i) the problems faced by Bengali Muslim migrants to East Pakistan, forced to uproot themselves from their Bengali socio-cultural past, which they shared with their Hindu neighbours; and (ii) the generation gap between the elderly (brought upon the past values of harmony) and the younger (confused by the disharmony of communal riots). Syed Badruddin sums up the two problems, by advising and warning his three young Hindu friends through a quote from the *Mahabharata*, where the author of the epic Vedavyasa tells his mother Satyavati: 'Mother, bad times lie ahead!'

The three friends finally land up in a village in East Pakistan—across a fluid border that was yet to be officially demarcated—without passports. They hear about a settlement of nomadic women dancers—a penal colony where they are confined as sex-slaves. One of the friends Satu visits the colony and comes across a woman called Moti. Her left arm is missing. She tells him that it was cut off with a chopper, when she was only five years old, by villagers who falsely accused her of stealing. Satu kisses the amputated end of her arm and says: 'I am a part of you :.. I will be born again and again here.'

By ending on this note in his novel *Khandita*, Samaresh Bose, through a striking literary bravura, turns the amputation of the arm of an individual woman as a metaphor for the territorial amputation of our country under partition, that for Bengali society meant the severing of its two arms—the east from the west.

Sumanta Banerjee

DISSEVERED

(Khandita)

Nineteen forty-seventh year of Christ. Fourteenth day of August. Evening. An industrial area of 24 Parganas lying about twenty miles to the north of Calcutta. An area full of jute mills and a few small factories, encircled by an extended slum quarter belonging to the poor and the working class of a country that is India or Bharat; dwellings tightly pressed against each other like cells of a beehive; filthy, unmetalled drains and an air heavy and poisonous with a fetid smell. Inside, the narrow lanes snake whichever way they want, though there is a firm line of brick-built buildings owned by the factories—more in the nature of unclean lodgings for the workers—along the road. Rows of toilets for both women and men employees where, at the same time, some twelve or sixteen women and men can—without cover—attend to nature's call. There are tea shops, some small grocery shops, and one or two minor streets that wander off to the main metallic road lined with big markets, stores and joints, selling country liquor. And it is from this thoroughfare that a little lane tunnels its way to the no less slummy prostitute quarters known as 'abode of the whores', though their proximity to the households of the poor and the labouring classes hardly distinguish these from the rest.

The industrial hub had come up on the in-between zone of the river Ganges (to its one side) and the rail road (to its other), running parallel to each other. The area was once—before laying of the rail tracks—a famous village marketplace with Kanchanpalli to its north and Ghugudangha to its south, skirting the river bank. Kanchanpalli is now Kanchrapara. It is the birthplace of the poet Ishwar Gupta. Years back, the British had built its arms factory in Ghugudangha. Clive had one of his houses here. Kumarhatta or Halisahar is but another name for what was once known as Haveli Parganas. It was famous during the age of the commercially successful Hindu–Buddhist imperial rulers of Saptagram. Garifa is the place of Keshab Sen's ancestral home. Jadav Chattopadhyay established a temple dedicated to Radhaballabh at the junction of Naihati and Kantalpara. Bankim Chattopadhyay, the novelist, was his son. Adjoining to it is Bhattapalli, in other words, Bhatpara, and somewhat resembling it Jagaddal Senpara where once, many years ago, Debendranath Thakur had come to perform the Brahmo rituals at the house of its main revenue officer (the Mazumdars). Then there are Nababgunj, Barrackpore, Agarpara of Nityananda, Peneti, Cossipore, and Barahnagar….

But let us, for the present, leave the topic of the settlements on the west bank of the Ganges river aside. The only reason for embarking upon the subject of the river's east bank now is because the railroads and the factories there had taken over villages belonging to many affluent Bengalis. In fact, it is now spread over the entire area, though at places, peeping from behind the industries, some villages still retain their presence as the abode of the Bengali middle-class, whilst carrying marks of time's tide. The area to the east of the rail tracks is still overwhelmingly rural. The rail factory of Kanchrapara has virtually drawn a line cordoning off the industrial region. The American Town Hall, named after Roosevelt, lies at its opposite end. The station at which the trains come to a halt is known to the locals as Chandmari. The aerodrome, the military barracks, and the arms dump all come under Nadia area. The Second World War has come to an end. The Roosevelt Town Hall is deserted. The army and the air force along with the arms, grenades, trucks, airplanes, and some cannon-fitted jeeps all have been transported elsewhere. Whatever has remained has been sold to the wartime contractors for a song. The contractors are now making huge profits bartering the goods left behind. The industries, in effect, have not succeeded in venturing beyond the 24 Parganas region.

The two of them were taking a pull at their cigarettes—Satu and Biju. Cheap fags. They stood leaning against the parapet on the west side of the terrace of Biju's two-storied house. The roar of the mike had begun since the early hours of the morning. Tomorrow would be August 15, the year 1947. The partition of the country had left the waters more muddy than transparent. There were so much doubts and suspicions regarding Khulna and Murshidabad in people's minds, so much murmuring and hissing about the fate of some areas surrounding Dinajpur in North Bengal. The ordinary people, of course, did not worry their heads over such matters, especially the non-Bengali folk working in the factories. The Hindi-speaking lot or the workers coming from India's south also did not have an iota of anxiety about the partition of the country. There was hardly any trace of the Punjabis or the Sindhis in the region. The average Bengali too did not have any headache about the problem. But the print media was full of all kinds of stories, and among the newspapers it was *Ittihad* that seemed to have become too audacious. But how many Hindu Bengali gentlemen actually read *Ittihad*? Therefore, it was not a surprise that all classes of people were drunk with joy at the prospect of an end to their 200 year-old state of bondage. There was a festive feeling everywhere—starting from the factories, rows of slums, markets, and the Bengali genteel areas. Melodious Bengali film songs along with patriotic music like *Kadam Kadam Baraye Ja* and *Bande Mataram* were being played throughout Bengali households. It was impossible to remain indifferent—the preparation for the next day—the advent of independence had already begun.

Yes, the preparations had taken off in shops, markets, and in people's homes—this precious independence coming after 200 years of slavery. India, or rather Bharat, was to gain freedom tomorrow, in exchange of decades of hardship, sorrow, humiliation, and sacrifice made in blood. Tomorrow would be a historic day—not only a day of joy. The tears that flowed freely from the eyes, while people embraced each other, were not only because of the memories of those unhappy times but also for the experience of unbounded happiness at freedom or *azadi*, the end of British imperialism! These were the words that floated out of the mike amidst the announcements of the inaugural ceremonies for the next day made by the political parties, along with repeated condemnation of British rule, the long years of imprisonment suffered by the heroes of independence. The sacrifice of millions of women and men, the killings, bloodshed were all remembered, as much as the names of those who gave their lives to the gallows. This joy and excitement at gaining freedom did not and could not remain suppressed. Rather, there was a sense of being transported in mad ecstasy. All kinds of preparation for the event were afoot at home and outdoors, in shops and markets, factories, slums, along the line of the company's habitation, in middle-class Bengali households.

'Dear friends, tomorrow at daybreak....'

The words came floating down from mikes fixed to cycle-rickshaws waving banners of three-coloured flags with Ashoka's wheel.

'These words make no sense,' Biju said with a laugh, blowing out a mouthful of cigarette smoke. 'The country is not becoming independent after 190 years, at daybreak tomorrow—it is happening at midnight, tonight....'

Satu roared with laughter. 'I knew you'd say something like that! Counting it down to 190 years instead of 200 years—and then freedom at midnight. The day does not begin at midnight in our country, dear friend. Read The *Statesman*. It mentions the midnight of August 14 as the eve of the independence day.'

'But the actual transfer of power is being made then, is it not?' Biju gave his fag a pull. 'It is not a mistake. I feel like broadcasting the news to everyone out there, saying, "Friends, inform all the factories, jute mills, press, and other industrial units that they should give the siren call at midnight tonight, light up the garlands of light, blow conch shells in people's homes, take processions out into the streets."'

'Come, let us sell our big idea to Tarakda—to Surenbabu at the least,' Satu said, pressing the end of the cigarette stub against the moss-laden parapet of the terrace.

Biju looked at Satu with amazement, pulling hard at the end of his cigarette butt, and almost at once, his fair-skinned face turned red; he stopped smoking and threw away what remained of the cigarette to one corner of the terrace and broke into a loud laughter. Satu joined him; he too laughed.

Tarakda stood for Tarak Bhattacharya, the local communist leader, also member of the district committee. As for Suren Basu, he was a veteran leader of the Congress Party, still very powerful, though no longer the secretary of its district committee. 'Both are going to beat me up,' said Biju. 'The programme for tomorrow is well nigh complete—everything arranged from the morning's march (*prabhat feri*) till the raising of the flag, garlanding the martyr's monument—and if I go now and say all this, both would think I am pulling their legs.'

Satu laughed loudly, shaking his mane. Biju joined in. Behind both was a two-storied house—an open terrace bereft of parapet but possessing an attic room with a tiled roof. There were two adolescent girls sitting at the eastern corner of the terrace, wearing knee-length frocks, and six young boys, about fifteen and sixteen, fixing a bamboo pole to the wall of the attic room with nails. It was clear they were preparing to fly the national flag on the morrow. Satu and Biju were not looking at them, though the boys were from out of the corner of their eyes.

There was a road to the west of Biju's house, asphalt-surfaced, unfit for plying big lorries or trucks, but not for small vehicles and cycle-rickshaws. The two were standing next to the parapet in one corner of the terrace. There was a *jamrul* tree at the other end of the road, and next to the tree a number of houses situated in close proximity to each other. The houses had only one storey each; in-between were a few brick-built buildings with tiled roofs. Some houses had boundary walls, others none. To the west of the houses was a land filled with a forest of deep green belladonna trees, sloping downwards till it reached the waters of the river Ganges. The river was now in ebb, its silted edges showing up. A few yellow-beaked, singing blackbirds were moving about the place, eating something scratched up. Encouraged, the doel birds also moved around them, dancing away. No bird or beast deigned to devour meko, a kind of minute insect similar to baby crabs. But there were also many more creatures like small shrimps prancing about the place. The birds devoured these.

The waters of the river in the month of Sraban were now a deep orange. It was the water of the melted snow cascading downwards. The mekos and the small prawns bred in such waters—millions of them are born and die. Therefore, the Ganges water carries a stinking smell. It is said that the hilsa fish prefers these waters, while the mekos and the prawns are mere messengers bringing in the news of the coming of the hilsa.

The sun had now gone behind the *jamrul* tree, its brightness peeping from the gaps among the thick foliage. The sky was cloudy, and the sun was not strong enough to penetrate the rather flippant clouds, except in places where they became visible through cracks in their midst. And there were streaks of reddish hue along the edges of the cracks. The clouds were reddish even where it was light and fleeting. It did not seem it was going to rain then; there had been light showers at noon.

The saffron-coloured water became even more red as the sun began to appear from behind the clouds; there was no breeze, though the atmosphere was not that hot or stuffy—not a puff of air about the place. All the boats of fishermen, angling in the river, had their sails unfurled; the boats were plying from the east to the west and seemed to move ever so slowly towards the south-east—almost without being noticed. One got the feeling that the dinghies were lying still in the waters. But if one looked up at the sky, one could see that the large flippant clouds were also not stationary. They were on the move as one could guess from their changing contours and scattered profiles. The clouds were moving in the westward direction.

'Okay, what are they thinking, those who are casting about their nets to catch fish in the waters? They are at it even today,' Satu's large eyes were transfixed on the Ganges river. 'Yet tomorrow—oh sorry! According to you, Bharat is getting its independence at midnight tonight, and sorry again, after 190 years.'

Satu smiled, baring his brightly polished teeth. Biju too laughed. Fair-skinned and about 5 feet 4 inches in height, a head full of hair, neither short nor dangling, though rather unruly, Satu was twenty-three years old, clean-shaven, with a skin as soft as girls. He was good-looking without doubt, sharp nose on a somewhat round face, large eyes with slightly brown pupils, bright yet deep in thought. Biju's proper name was Saurindranath Mitra. He had a reputation for being a bright and intelligent student, had passed out with a First in MA in Ancient History, but his teeth were not glistening bright as Satu's. He did not chew betel leaf and smoked only occasionally, at the most four or five times when he was very happy. Today he seemed to be smoking again. 'Have I said anything wrong by quoting those figures—190....'

'I refuse to argue with you,' Satu entreated with palms folded. 'You are carrying memories of the year 1757 in your head, the Battle of Plassey. You haven't said anything wrong—everything ended with that war and now we are in the year 1947.'

Biju was wearing a pyjama and panjabi. He kicked Satu's blue trousers lightly above the knee.

'You, *shala* jolly fellow, why do you hit me below my belt saying 190 years?' Biju bit his tongue and said, 'Lor, I've gone and kicked the son of a Brahmin!'

'What's even worse is your calling me *shala*,' Satu laughed, making his eyes big.

Biju said, 'That I will do all over and over again, it's good. Will call you jolly fellow, bastard, motherfucker, and what not! You stupid!'

'Leave all that!' Satu almost begged folding his palms. 'You've made enough display of your skills—you are capable of saying anything and everything, but you don't, and you feel bad when we come out with those swear words. But today—oh! I understand you are in good mood because of independence.'

Biju shook his head vigorously, 'But, of course, like the saying, when one is happy, the mind turns into *tabula rasa*, emptied out of all its discontents. It is how I feel now. There's not a jot of inhibition impeding my thoughts.'

'That's why I was saying everyone is drunk with happiness because the country is becoming independent. And those fishermen who are carrying on with their job, do they have no sense of joy in their hearts?'

'Of course they do,' Biju laughed, removing a flock of hair from his brows. 'But why do you forget one thing? It's not enough to revel in merriment; one must have some dough in one's sack too. How can Satyesh Chatterjee be oblivious of it all?'

'That's because Satyesh Chatterjee has borrowed rupees fifty today,' Satu laughed and said. 'It's only the middle of the month, and I have already overspent. I don't live your lives, dear. I don't have a rich parent, and I have been thrown out of the house.'

Biju moved the orbs of his eyes like girls, 'You are a fat arse! Why should they turn you out of the house, an offspring of a gentleman? You refused to study, then got married to the lower-caste Kayastha girl at this young age. If, instead, you had looked for a job, you could have lived a rich and comfortable life. But no you had to go and fall in love, get married and move out, and become a householder at this tender age of twenty-three, and now you are also the father of a boy....'

'Now you are pontificating like a teacher of morals,' Satu puckered his brows and gave Biju a glare. 'You applauded me when I fell in love and then got married; you told folks that you were so proud of your friend, and to Pratima, gushing, that she was incomparable when you came home! And now you behave as if you are the guardian of Satu Chatterjee?'

Biju's giggle sounded like that of a girl. 'How easily your mood is spoilt by saying all these things. But for heaven's sake, don't repeat all this to Pratima. Actually, I was pulling your leg. You are different, you can do so many things, a born poet, the greatest and best poet among us, the youth.'

'Are you making fun of me?' Satu's face darkened. 'Not a single collected book of poems has come out thus far.'

Biju screwed up his brows, a tone of astonishment in his voice. He said, 'How many poems have you written till now that you are thinking of the publication of collected poems? What I mean is, you may have written quite a few, but how many of them have got printed? I think about a dozen in some journals and newspapers. And already Bishnu Dey and Buddhadeb Bose have praised you. What better luck can you have? Let a couple of years pass. I am sure you'll publish collected works of who knows how many of them—even you cannot know that! And have you forgotten Bishnu Dey's words or the letter that Buddhadeb had written about your poetic efforts that you had so much talent and promise? But what is this, Satu? Why are you behaving like a child?'

Drops of tears appeared and were about to fall from Satu's orbs. He put his two arms around Biju's neck and, like a child, pressed his face against his shoulders. Biju drew him in with a big hug. His voice too sounded slightly harsh and broken, 'Rascal, you are an idiot. Today's the eve of independence day, is it not?'

'And at midnight tonight....' Satu lifted his wet face from Biju's shoulders and smiled. Biju's eyes were also red and tearful.

Both looked at each other and broke into laughter. Hearing this sudden loud commotion of their laughter, the girls and boys in the terrace behind again gave them a stare. Their eyes betrayed suspicion and curiosity. Were Satuda and Bijuda making fun of them for all the effort they were making to fly the national flag? No, that cannot be, because both of them were now locked in embrace, gazing at each other's face.

The sun was again peeping from the cracks in the fleeting westward-moving clouds in the sky. The sun which had sloped further down and fallen on the ground below was now sending fire-like beams through the apertures in the cloud mass covering the entire firmament. Satu brought out a packet of crushed cigarettes from the pocket of his blue trousers. And a box of matches. He took out one and gave it to Biju. 'That's enough. We'll both pull at one, you hold it. I'll merely take a draw.'

'But didn't you say you'd buy some when you come away from your place?'

'I will, but I don't feel like smoking a whole cigarette right at this moment.'

Satu put the packet back into his pocket and lighted a cigarette striking a match. He had large eyes, but one could not say he had a snub nose, though it was neither very sharp nor pointed. A head full of curly locks, he was taller than Biju by a few inches, perhaps 5 feet 6 or 7 inches in height, and with a dark complexion. Big dark eyes, the pupils bright and deep, a longish face still soft, not clean-shaven, with a pair of moustache, his body fit and cultivated as one could see by its looks. He pulled hard a couple of times at the cigarette and then extended it to Biju. Biju took hold of it, took a look of its end, then turned to Satu, gave a laugh, and pressed it against his mouth and gave a pull.

'My mouth is not full of saliva,' Satu said, 'unlike Gora's. But why is he not here? Sleeping away?' Satu shook his head in disbelief, a streak of amusement on his face. 'Gora said he would eat meat everyday from today, so delighted was he, but prone to oversleep, he is. But see, he will appear all of a sudden with a bag full of new stories to tell.'

'Whenever you talk about Gora, you bring up his habit of rumour-mongering,' Satu laughed. 'But the stories about Suhrawardy are not lies or mere gossip. It was Tarakda who had talked about it, coming straight from Calcutta. Tarakda is not one who would talk rubbish. Besides, he would not say something like that about Suhrawardy, the leader of Muslim League.'

Biju pointed the cigarette in Satu's direction, blew out a puff of smoke, and said, 'I didn't say that Tarakda lied. But Suhrawardy had gone to Darjeeling and talked to Governor Casey; he had told him that he will see to it that the 24 Parganas, Barrackpore, Basirhat all came under the ambit of East Pakistan. None of this was ever printed in the papers, only Tarakda had indicated it. Casey had said that both Calcutta and Darjeeling were going to be declared as common cities of the whole of Bengal province. But even this news was not published as Casey's declaration. One will never know the difference between truth and falsehood in all these cogitations, but everybody is aware of the League's "Keep Calcutta" movement.'

'I think actually Suhrawardy must have revealed his daydreams (illusions) to Casey. Tarakda is rather thick with the League. Everybody knows about the bonhomie between Suhrawardy and the communists. Didn't Gora say he had read all about it in the *Ittihad*? Casey's remark about Barrackpore, Basirhat, Bhangar, and Barasat going to East Pakistan has come from reliable sources. Ugh! Gora was so scared. Remember how teary he looked, as if about to breakdown?'

'Now you are laughing, so am I. But it was terrible—rumours of those days! My mind too got consumed by fear. How can the Barrackpore subdivision go to East Pakistan? Besides papers like *Azad, Star of India, Morning News*, all the Muslim League papers were continually making claim over Calcutta.'

'This was kind of spreading fake news. The Boundary Commission and the real League ought to know what is the actual situation.' Satu blew out a ring of smoke. 'Suhrawardy wanted to preserve his image among the Muslims of Bengal. But I cannot understand why Huq Sahib was going along with him, knowing everything! I was taken by surprise to hear someone like him making the demand for the inclusion of Calcutta. When the partition was being effected on the basis of majority–minority population and Calcutta was a Hindu majority area, wouldn't Huq Sahib know that? Whatever people might say, I refuse to regard Huq Sahib as communal.'

'See, you are getting me mad again,' Biju laughed. 'I don't know how you claim you know Huq Sahib that well! Gora would've given you a fitting reply had he been here. Come on, let me take a pull.'

'Why not finish the rest?' Satu held out the cigarette to Biju. 'What do you mean by asking if I know Huq Sahib that well? You've spent all your time cramming lessons, but I started reading the newspapers ten years earlier to this day. Huq Sahib is a genuine Bengali leader; he may be a Muslim, but he is greater than many Hindu Bengali leaders. He has joined Muslim League only lately. That's why I say, how can a person who has the whole history of Bengal in his grasp, a leader like him, carry on a movement like "Keep Calcutta"?

Satu took another pull and let out a puff of smoke. 'Don't know why you consider Suhrawardy to be so mean-minded. You yourself say he's friendly with the communists. He is no less intelligent than Huq Sahib. Doesn't matter, maybe I don't commit to memory all that the newspaper conveys, but I do think that Huq Sahib overdoes things. He sounds so melodramatic, beating his chest again and again and calling himself a Bengali. But how is it that this Bengal tiger (Sher-i-Bengal) Fazlul Huq's mouth was sealed when the time had come for asking for the prisoners of the '42 Movement to be set free? Yet, he is not only the chief minister of Bengal, but also its home minister.'

'See Biju, one can't argue over in-built prejudices,' Satu turned his face towards the river. 'One can always discover all kinds of faults in a person one wants to belittle, regard the expression of genuine emotions, as dramatic. You say he sounds melodramatic—that's his virtue, his power—that's how I regard it. No matter if a person be the head of a household, a leader of the masses, or the charioteer of the state, he has to have power, that's his obsession, his *idée fixe*. I am not saying that Huq Sahib was absolutely indifferent to power. But didn't he announce the decision to unconditionally free the thirty seven, thirty eight prisoners at the state assembly when Gandhi was himself trying for that? Then it was Herbert himself who made him the chief minister, while both Suhrawardy and Nazimuddin knowing all this were trying to stab him at the back. Herbert was something. In those days, all the civilians, police officers, and bureaucrats were at his beck and call. But even so, Herbert understood that Huq carried more weight (had more stronghold) among the ordinary people than either Suhrawardy or Nazimuddin. It was Herbert who put aside the question of the release of the prisoners of the '42 Movement. Then came the news of the atrocities committed on women by the soldiers in Noakhali. Because a Bengali Muslim magistrate had registered a complaint, he was promptly removed from office. Huq had himself run to Noakhali and had to face the whole officialdom, both the big and small officers ere he reached the Noakhali Station. All had one thing to say, 'Sir, you are not allowed to go there.' But suppose he had forced his way in? What would have happened? He would have been lifted and packed back in a train to Calcutta. A similar situation obtained in Midnapore. Huq had run there learning of the atrocities on the forty-two prisoners and was sent back to Calcutta in a similar fashion. He was not allowed to enter Midnapore. He was circumspect and therefore did not insist, and would have been insulted had he forced himself in. And the papers would have carried the whole story in big print. Would the Congress Party come and stood next to him in that situation? Made him a hero? Not a chance. He would have had to return swallowing the humiliation. Then he was struck with fear. The Japanese were gradually making their way to India, having conquered Burma and Malaysia. Herbert could not trust Huq any further. Even the Bengali Hindu leaders were not in favour of him. It was for Suhrawardy and Nazimuddin a piece of good luck. The British wanted to rid the feelings of hatred for the British among the Bengalis; they knew that Fazlul Huq was not capable of that. Therefore, the Hindu leaders gradually removed themselves from his side at the beck and call of no less a person than Nazimuddin, who soon, with the backing of the British, assumed the position of the home minister. As for the question of the release of the prisoners, Subhash Bose's call was wafting in the air. Nazimuddin had taken leave from work a few days before the actual release of the prisoners. Sir Bijoyprasad Singh Roy had taken over the duties of the home ministry in his absence. The amiable gentleman however loved to sleep with his eyes open. Taking advantage of that, a British officer went like a thief to Herbert and requested him to repeal the act of setting the prisoners free. Herbert did just that. The liberation of the prisoners never came about. Now come to think of it, was Nazimuddin's leave taking, Bijoyprasad's slumber—as if he didn't know anything—and Governor Herbert's cancellation of the release of the prisoners coincidental? Nalinaksha Sanyal had let out the name of the British officer—some Porter....'

Biju was listening to Satu, bending his frame over the parapet. By that time, the cigarette had burnt down to its last bit and was scorching his fingertips. He pressed it against the walls of the parapet and threw it on the road below. He tried to laugh, and wanted to say something amusing to Satu so that he too laughed. But looking at Satu's absent-minded looks, peering far away at the river Ganga, he could not come up with any amusing talk, although he tried to say feebly, 'Satyesh Chatterjee has turned so serious, ain't he?'

'You can say that,' Satu turned to him and smiled. 'Of course, the release of prisoners that was to be in 1943 actually took place in

1946. And Suhrawardy was then the chief minister. The prisoners of Chittagong Armoury Raid were also released. That was why Suhrawardy and the communists became so friendly. He has a progressive mind, this Suhrawardy, an admirer of Jamini Roy, also his patron. But to my mind, the strain of an obnoxious destructive diplomacy of the British runs through his veins. The proof? August 16, the last year. How can people forget that even the fair-minded Muslims had come out in support of Jinnah in response to Suhrawardy's call for "Direct Action". And that call was for the creation of Pakistan and against the British government. And what did Nazimuddin tell the Calcutta Muslims? Our *jehad* or resolve is not against the government but against the Hindus. The so-called progressive Suhrawardy ordered all the government offices to remain closed on August 16. The reason? So that no officer gets hurt in the event of any riot if they are indoors. But why only they? The whole of Calcutta was to be shut down. To oppose the rule would have been to oppose Pakistan. Suhrawardy was not playing with fire, he was playing a game to its finish with a cool head. And the August 16 riots of last year have proved all over again that the Hindus and Muslims have to remain separate and apart. Whatever the purpose of the riots for whosoever it was meant, was served. The country's leaders' wishes, however, remained unfulfilled. What the British had wanted is going to be fulfilled tomorrow. I am happy that no matter all the mess they've created, at least the country will become independent. But remember Biju, the release of the prisoners has not as yet been affected. I don't wish to mention other aspects of Suhrawardy because, I think, whatever grand illusions he might have must now have ended. Where is Suhrawardy Sahib today, Biju?'

Biju said with a tone of surprise, 'Why, in Calcutta, of course?'

'Yes, in Beliaghata. And why is that?'

'To be near Gandhi.'

'And why? Why is he now next to Gandhi?'

'To save the Bengali Muslims, that's his greatness. When all other Muslim leaders have run off to Pakistan or are making arrangement to go, the only Muslim leader who stays behind is Suhrawardy, not only to save the Muslims in Calcutta but in the whole of India.' Biju suddenly found himself in possession of firm reasoning; he became rather excited.

'But, for that, why must the last year's Bengal chief minister go to Gandhiji now?'

There was not a trace of harshness in Satu's voice. Rather, a mix of emotions, both sad and happy.

'I have no personal enemity against Suhrawardy Sahib. I have been talking about his activities of the last two years. Today, you are talking of Hindu–Muslim amity along with Prafulla Ghosh taking Nazimuddin with you, but couldn't you have—a person of your stature—taken Nazimuddin to task last August? The same war-mongering Nazimuddin who had declared, "Our fight is not against the Indian government, but against the Hindus." You did not even utter a word in protest then. Never mind, the government then belonged to the League Party. And will you keep shut all the government offices on the days the League Party has programmes? What do you think? Wouldn't the Hindus take a fright at this? Become suspicious? Why did you force them to participate in your Direct Action melee? You built a rocket only to turn its wick in the opposite direction. Your satisfaction lasted only for three days. Didn't you know that no matter how many Pathan police officers you have at your disposal, or how many officers of the police post you transfer out overnight, and introduce Muslims into the area, Calcutta is actually the city of the Hindus? Your rocket went up blazing at one moment, but soon got knocked down and fell. That's but natural. What could the British police or the military and the Pathan troops do when the Hindus jumped into the fray in double revenge. Everything went up in flames. To make things even, riots took place in Noakhali. To settle scores with Noakhali, fires broke out in Bihar. I wouldn't know if Suhrawardy was that sharp or far-seeing, or that he did what he did with a cool head to create a country called Pakistan. No matter what, Biju, I don't feel like talking about all these unpleasant things. While we thought of ourselves as somewhat of the Left, and shouted aloud about the getting together of Gandhi and Jinnah or of the union of Muslim League and the Congress, that gentleman was like a incompetent manufacturer producing fake fireworks.'

The fleeting clouds in the western sky were continuously breaking up, scattering all over the horizon. The sun going down even further westward, the dense mass overhead becoming fluffy and light. And the nude sky was now gradually showing up as red, like the tips of flames. The saffron-coloured water cascading from the mountains was in a reddish spate. Its tint fell upon the Ganges surface, on the sails of the dinghies, and on the torsos of the fishermen. To the front, the leaves of the *jamrul* tree carried the same colour. Red light streaked in through the apertures in the foliage, and fell on the visages of Biju and Satu. 'Must say that both the metaphor of the rocket as well as the comparison with the incompetent manufacturer of fireworks is apt! Though not communal, you have probably a sharp critical poem against the leader rotating in your head. I am reminded of the poems of Samar Sen,' Biju intervened, 'You so and so … '

'Come, say it. Why stop, motherfucker? Isn't that what you want to say?'

'I see, now you are talking! Saurindra Mitra or Biju Mitra's mouth is full of obscene words.'

'I had already said that, but seriously you have excelled even yourself in your chatter.'

'Even so, how can you compare so and so with so and so?'

'I haven't lied, I swear by the Mother of God!' Biju broke into a laugh, though trying to sound serious.

'*Mairie*, your mouth is full of filth today, starting from *shala* to *mairie*! And yet when we say something, you look as if you've seen a ghost. You can't stand all the vulgar words uttered by the low caste! Go and wash your mouth clean in the purifying waters of the Ganges.'

'I won't. Today I am one of the low-born. Today, I understand that all the reasoning does not stand; it is circumstances and environment that make a man what he is. Yet, there is so much pretension all around us and one can see that as well. Why do you think all our notions are coming apart today? Because we've become free—it is Independence Day. I will talk like the city's lumpen proletariat, who ply away their time seated on the raised terrace in front of people's houses. Why won't I?'

'Not a good sign, Biju,' Satu smiled. 'You are changing your mind too rapidly. May be you will think differently after you've hardly uttered this.'

'Will see to that, but now let me say what I want. Where's the bastard, Gora? Why isn't he here as yet?'

Both looked at each other and broke into a loud laughter. The girls and boys on the terrace behind again gave them suspicious looks. But Biju could not help continuing with the topic. He said, 'But Satu, you've forgotten about Suhrawardy's opposition to the "Keep Calcutta" campaign. He had declared Dacca as the capital of East Pakistan last June, didn't he? And didn't your Huq Sahib then give a contrary speech?'

'He did,' Satu smiled again, 'but why bring up all those topics now, Biju? Huq Sahib was compelled to speak differently the day he left the Praja Krishak Party and joined the League. But I will say that he never, at any given time, speaks in contrary voices. Suhrawardy was very much there during the "Keep Calcutta" campaign, not to mention Nazimuddin. And also, why forget that it was him, Suhrawardy, who had gone to Darjeeling to meet Casey in order to plead for the inclusion of Calcutta, Barrackpore, Barasat, Basirhat, and Bhangar in East Pakistan? Casey had advised him to carry on the campaign. That's why I say, Suhrawardy's grand illusions have evaporated, Biju. *One has to return again/in the direction the river Ajoy took/when flowing with Ganges on the holy Sankranti* (the last day of the month). I am reminded of the poet Jayadev's analogy. Like him, Suhrawardy has to let Ajoy River flow in the direction of Ganga. I am reminded here of Rabindranath's poem 'Rupnarayaner Kule', but I really doubt if Suhrawardy has the ability to distinguish the false from the true. Only yesterday we got to know from the newspapers about the Boundary Commissions Reports, the declaration that Calcutta, 24 Parganas, Darjeeling, Jalpaiguri have all come under West Bengal. Yet the fate of Maldah, Nadia, and Dinajpur are still hanging in the air. We know next to nothing about Murshidabad. What magic will make Suhrawardy learn that the "Keep Calcutta" slogan is a big bluff? Learn he must! What's the situation in

Calcutta today? The Bihari Muslims of Calcutta are being sent back to Bihar. Are they all bestowing their blessings on Suhrawardy? Have the jaws of those helpless Muslims sent in hordes in special trains to East Pakistan from Canal West Road slackened? Today, Calcutta is under curfew. Everybody thought it will be lifted tomorrow, but it won't be. Rather, the period of curfew has been extended by a few more days. And tomorrow is also the country's Independence Day! Do you think Suhrawardy is experiencing some kind of a blow of the conscience that makes him run from the communists to other parties so that Gandhiji is requested to remain in Calcutta? Why is he himself running all over the city? Just think, three Hindus were killed in Entally only three days ago! Can you imagine Muslims being pulled down from a train from the South and slaughtered? And today some sense has dawned on you, the great leader that you are! And you declare that you will fast tomorrow with Gandhiji. But would the reasons for your mutual fasting be one and the same? You wanted Pakistan and have got it. Gandhiji did not wish the country to be divided, that's why this day can only be one of smile filled with tears for him. He has accepted tomorrow's independence by fasting. Biju … '

Was Satu's throat trembling? His voice getting choked? Biju pressed his hand and called out, 'Satu.'

'I am leaving for Calcutta tomorrow,' Satu uttered the words as if taking an oath.

'Calcutta! Whatever for?'

'Beliaghata. I am going there to see Gandhiji. I feel like touching his feet—just this once!'

'Satu-u-u?' Biju's voice rose in amazement. 'You-u-u want to touch Gandhiji's feet! You—the sympathizer of the Communist Party, an upholder of their principles. And you want to go to Gandhiji?'

'I want to,' Satu was unable to control his emotions. 'It's true that I'm a supporter of the Communist Party, but I cannot lie to myself, to you, or to Gora. I have had to swallow the theory of the existence of Hindustan/Pakistan, but my heart is about to break. The one thing that has darkened whatever joy I may have had at the advent of independence is the defeat of us both, the Hindus and the Muslims. They are not going to leave this country without dividing us forever. In such a situation, who do we have but Gandhiji? I know, for you this is a matter of disbelief, but Biju, I am helpless! At home, Pratima is sewing up a flag of three-coloured cloths. The first thing for me to do when I wake up tomorrow is to hoist the flag. You and Gora must come. Have to stand on the line in the market to buy meat the minute the flag goes up. Whatever people might think or say, after all tomorrow is Independence Day. Everyone will feast on all kinds of food, good and bad. I am not saying I am not happy. Tell me, does a person who is suffering from illness also not feel happy at times? My situation is somewhat similar.'

Biju gazed at Satu's face. He was himself much better in study, and had quite a reputation in the neighbourhood. Rather, Satu was not liked much; he had fallen in love at this young age and married a Kayastha girl against his family's wishes. He had become a father of a boy at a young age. Biju's father disliked Satu, yet Biju was proud of his friend, almost besotted, you can say. He took his hand and pressed it hard.

'Satu, how swiftly you change your argument! This is where you win. Your real obsession is not Suhrawardy, it's something different, and in this there's no difference between us; we think the same way. We have had to, after all this time, accept the two-nation theory for which the country has been severed. What do you think, am I not suffering because of it? I had read in *Ittihad* that what makes the Musims happy, makes the Hindus unhappy. Even the faces of our leftist friends, who have been renting the air shouting slogans for Gandhi-Jinnah unity not so long ago, are downcast. The topic had come up on May 16, in the context of the Cabinet Mission's plans. Both the Congress and the League had accepted the plan. I wonder if Tarakda remembers all that; don't know what Surenbabu thinks either. The *Ittihad* perhaps trusts no Hindu, save Sarat Bose. But do you think I can accept the division of the country? Me, a student of history? I get frightened by your talk, Satu. Hope tomorrow doesn't turn out to be unlucky for us.'

'But we are now free, it's my mistake, I mean at midnight—tomorrow,' Satu began to laugh. 'We will become free tonight at midnight and together fight against all evils.'

Biju still looked serious, his face downcast. Then, suddenly hearing Satu's words, it lighted up, like the sunlight in autumn. 'I beg your pardon—what does midnight mean? Haven't you seen in the papers that today at midnight the Indian parliament will assume control of ruling the country? And almost immediately, the British soldiers would lose their jobs? Tonight, at midnight, the Governor's house will be observing an unique historical ceremony. Understand, you ass? Tonight, at midnight! And tomorrow morning, you'll listen to the declaration.'

'And the cannons at Fort William will be booming,' Satu again took out a packet of ciggies from his trouser pocket. 'By Mary, the Mother of God, I'm so sad. I won't be able to hear all that from where I now live. Only see the squadron of war planes waft over our heads, that is, if they deign to fly in this direction, but they won't. Come, let's both go to Calcutta early morning tomorrow.'

Biju shook his head and laughed, 'Everybody, just about everybody will be wanting to be in Calcutta. We'll stay right here, but if you so wish, you may go to Beliaghata once....'

Dying to smoke, Satu brought out a cigarette. 'But you and Gora are going to have your meal at my place this afternoon. You can go there in the evening; as a matter of fact, I myself am thinking of going....But have to salute the new government for forbidding to light up the city in festivity because of the sadness at the country's partition. Come, take a pull at the fag!'

Satu pushed a ciggie into Biju's mouth ere he extended his palm. He lighted it up striking a match. 'Have only one left now. Won't Gora come? Come, let's go out.'

Biju blew out a ring. The western sky looked darker in the thick haze of the smoke. The tip of the cigarette had a reddish glow.

'*Swapna O Sadhana*' (To dream and to arduously endeavour!) Shouting exultantly, Gaur arrived on the terrace, almost dancing away. Gora was his pet name, almost as tall as Satu, twenty-four years of age, a striped half-shirt over a dhoti, worn tightly tucked between the legs; hair neatly parted and tightly pressed from the back down to the front, now a bit unruly because of the movement of the fingers. A pair of moustache trim and neat, a slim body, without any sign of fat, for which he is sad as he wants to put on some weight. A sharp nose and slanted eyes, a shade or two fairer than Satu, but compared with Biju, somewhat darker. He came striding through the open door and neared the parapet to the west of the terrace. 'Sandhya Rani and Paresh Banerjee, direction Agradut. The film is going to be released here tomorrow—must see it, 6 o'clock show and....'

'Not interested! Biju blew out a whiff of smoke. 'Those feminine-looking males are not fit to be cast as heroes. Look at Gary Cooper. He is old enough to be Paresh's father and he can still act like a romantic hero. Have you seen *For Whom the Bell Tolls*? Now people compare Paresh Bannerjee's looks with Durgadas Bannerjee!'

'Whack,' Gora spat out, giving a big stare. He looked at Satu in amazement.

Satu winked and said, 'Beware, Biju is in a foul mood today. Who knows what he's going to come out with….'

'Really!' Gora's eyes gaped in astonishment and disbelief. 'The devil quoting the scriptures, is it? Because I say so and so, you come after me?'

Biju looked serious; he blew out a puff of smoke. 'You can't say whatever you want; you must have the capacity. If you cannot utter the right words at the right time, making the correct intonation, it will all sound vile, obscene. If you don't have this much sense, you can only make vulgar remarks—*Swapna O Sadhana*, you so and so!'

'*Uff*,' Gora started as if he had been stabbed in the chest. He looked at Satu again, nonplussed.

Satu laughed, 'Why are you looking at me? He's saying what he wants to. And now, at past 11 o' clock, with what news have you come to us, dear Gaur Ghosh? Sandhya Rani and Paresh Bannerjee, *Swapna O Sadhana*? You could have mentioned the name of Pramathesh Barua at the least. Why not talk about Pahari Sanyal? Is Kananbala dead and gone? If nothing, at least you could have alluded to Dhiraj Bhattacharya.'

'It's my fault, dears!' Gora begged with folded palms, his nostrils trembling. He gave a look that could kill. 'Should have taken Ingrid Bergman's name, instead of rattling off all those.'

'You will, you can. Come, have a fag,' said Biju, extending his lighted-up cigarette to Gora almost at that minute. What a devastating smile there was on his face, his tender skin fair and beautiful as girls, though his voice was soft and harmless.

'I have some,' Gora brought out a blue-coloured packet of cigarettes from the hind pocket of his striped shirt. It was a large packet with the words 'Capstan' written in gold, and somewhat below, the words 'magnum size' in small print, and even further below, above the name of the company on the folded cable of the ship, a picture of the captain, his eyes on Satu.

A smile spread all over Satu's unshaven face, and his eyes danced in curiosity and merriment. 'Capstan, this instead of bidi from Ratan's shop? Really, now no one can deny that the country is becoming independent at midnight tonight. Today is the fourteenth. Where did you collect your salary?'

'Why should I go to receive my pay today?' Gora pulled at his steel-sharp, drooping moustache, looking at Biju from out of the corner of his eye, and said, 'Someone has given me a present. Take one.' He offered one to Satu. Biju went on smiling the same way with looks that can kill. 'Such luck! Why was I not born as the son of Hari Ghosh, the ever-charitable cowherd. It's a present from Ingrid Bergman, no less.'

'Objection,' Gora retorted, his nostrils flaring, appearing overdramatic. 'I don't like the habit of abusing someone by calling his father names.'

Biju knew how to fester a raw wound. He could hit Gora where it hurt the most. Actually, he loved to tease the bloke. Gora's quick temper amused him; his overdramatic reactions encouraged him to do this even more. Biju's sense of fun infected Satu as well, though he was more circumspect. But it was not that, at times, Satu too did not try to tease Biju, calling him a low-caste. Biju, however, could not be provoked; he could laugh all that off. He threw the burnt-out cigarette in the middle of the terrace, and hurriedly snatched one of Gora's—so hurriedly that Gora didn't have the time to take away his hand. Biju held the cigarette next to his nose and sniffed, 'Harendra Chandra Ghosh, meaning my Haren Uncle from Goalpara, is someone I respect a great deal, but teasing one's friend is a separate matter. I accept your objection and am soliciting your forgiveness. But Satu, just take a sniff. I cannot find a trace of Ingrid Bergman's aroma in it.'

'So you are even familiar with Ingrid Bergman's fragrance? Who knows whether Ingrid crawled inside Gary Cooper's quilt or Sauren Mittir's?' Gora's pair of moustache now stiffened up like a pair of bows.

There was a sound of protest in Satu's voice, 'I don't like the kind of things you are saying about the heroine of *For Whom the Bell Tolls*. You simply cannot make such remarks about the mistress of the revolutionary anti-fascist Roberto, fighting against Franco.'

'Correct,' Biju shook his head vigorously, but there was no trace of discomfiture or regret in his smile. Rather, a note of amusement was visible in the smile.

'The idea of a bodily smell is vulgar, I agree. I, of course, didn't mean anything like that, but it is hard to forget someone like Ingrid Bergman. I will, if, why if, I must when I go to Europe or America see Ingrid Bergman in person. Try to talk to her. She is the only one, among all the cinema heroines I have seen to this day, fit to be in love with. It's only Ingrid, it is only she I have fallen in love with. I don't care what people are going to say about it; she is in my dreams and in my imagination.'

Gora bit his tongue and interrupted, 'Leave all that, it's enough….I must say that the respectable and educated gentleman, that is Sauren Mittir, is today actually laying bare his heart, pouring out his emotions … ' He turned to Satu and smiled. 'I have also heard the names of Bette Davis, Susan Hayward, and Lili Palmer so many times. Leave all that; all that imagining is platonic love. There is not a whiff of sex in any love for the heroines of bioscope dear, especially when it comes to Biju Mittir.'

'Who says there is no whiff of sex? Of course, there is a lot of it,' Biju laughed. 'Would I ever say that I will go and see Ingrid Bergman when I visit the foreign shores no matter what? And even if I don't manage to see anybody else, if there isn't.'

'True, no doubt, when the case is of Sauren Mittir, the darling son of the multimillionaire Sachin Mittir.' Gora puckered his eyes, trying to look forbidding. 'You'll have to hunt from one end of the earth to the other to look for a beautiful daughter of a *kayet kulin* (exclusive caste) household, maybe then the heroine of films might appear trivial. Come Biju, light a match. How long are you going to keep the cigarette dangling from your fingers?'

Biju took up the cigarette and said, 'Only we haven't yet got to know who has presented you with this packet of Capstans. Sudhaboudi, perhaps, pleased with her son's private tutor, has today presented him with a pack of cigarettes.' Satu turned his face away from Biju and gave Gora a meaningful look. There was a hint of amusement in his puzzled eyes, a trace of smile around the mouth of an unshaven face.

Gora's brows stiffened; his pair of moustache became taut like a pair of swords. But almost at once, he broke into a peal of laughter. Looking at Biju, he said, 'And now say, whose smell do you discern in the packet of cigarettes?'

'Oh, my God! I can't—I simply cannot say all that rubbish about Sudhaboudi,' Biju touched his head with his palms in obeisance. 'Although all kinds of people in the city say all kinds of things about Sudhaboudi, the most beautiful Jezebel in our midst, nevertheless I have great regard for her. So many men have tried to cheat Prakash Mukherjee—that dark-skinned, mad husband of hers—mob him of all his money, the nephews of Prakash Mukherjee not excluding. But could they? Sudhaboudi is formidable in these senses too. She has made them all lick the dust. And not to mention, all the casanovas in the neighbourhood who have in some way or the other offered their love to Prakash Mukherjee's beautiful wife. Everybody knows about this. It's the city's open secret. But I will not say anything bad about Sudhaboudi or tolerate any other person saying it.'

Gora's large elongated eyes bore a distracted look. He was gazing at the sky in the west, listening to Biju. The western corner of the sky was gradually losing its reddish colour and taking on the hue of dusky grey—as if dried-up blood that has been lying for a long period on the open earth. He turned his head when Biju ended his chatter. There was not an iota of taunt or reprimand in his expression. Rather, he smiled as if in gratitude, and along with this, a cover of sadness, like a light mist, wafted over his face. 'Yes, it is Sudhaboudi who's given this to me. Satu has said the right thing, but not to me alone, she has given presents to you as well, mentioning both your names. She said, "Tell them this is from me",' and Gora took out two more Capstan packets from another pocket of his shirt. He gave a mischievous smile now, 'What did you two think—that I would filch your presents? Her gift to you? I could never have done that, any gift from her—but yes, would have played around a bit. Anyway, come on, take....' He held out the two packets towards them.

Now Biju and Satu were smiling all over again, a different kind of smile this. No light-hearted mirth, wit, or waggery; a real sense of pleasure and amazement was there, as also some regard and gratitude.

People in the city gossiped a lot about Gora's relationship with Sudhaboudi, and said bad things. Of course, the source of all the small talk was the Mukherjee household; it had spread from there to elsewhere. Prakash Mukherjee's elder brother Sukumar Mukherjee and his sons didn't stop at spreading all kinds of canards about their aunt. They warned Gora and abused him openly. Gora was somewhat hot-tempered; there were times when, maddened, he had confronted Sukumar Mukherjee and his sons openly and they had run away in shame. Gora was to them no longer a libertine, or a debauche, but an anti-social. And who can take on a thug? After all, they were gentlemen!

Gora did pass his MA in Bengali, but his results were not good. Though not a bad student, he was not able to obtain even a second class. His elder brother had travelled to Scotland and Dundee. He was a mechanical apprentice in a jute mill from his adolescence, a kind of trainee you can say. In the jute mills of those days, people referred to the likes of him as 'mistri boy'. Gora's father was also a well-established mistri boy of a jute mill, but the sahibs referred to him as an engineer. Whatever work the mechanic could not perform was accomplished by Haru Ghosh. In fact, Haru Ghosh's job was to set aright whichever machine in the factory failed to work. He was borrowed by other companies if needed. He could take care of both mechanical failures and other kinds of crisis. Everyone would be struck with awe and admiration for him. Gora's brother had also started his career as the mistri boy of the jute mill, though he had school education. The authorities of the company sent him to their own factory in Dundee, Scotland, observing his skills. He became the town's first 'England returned', in other words, '*bilayet pherat*' Gurudas Ghosh. Now he was the company's chief mechanical officer. He was the first among people with his kind of education in the factory who lived in one of the palatial company houses. Gora was also ambitious, but he couldn't achieve much. Biju had. He was preparing for his PhD exams and had a good reputation in the academic circles. His professors had him in their sight, and so did many others, such as the local political parties. Biju, however, had leanings towards the Communist Party.

Gora was now thinking of studying for an MA in English. He didn't appear to have interest in any particular political ideology, though he was associated with the group that indulged in communist bashing, at the beginning of the year before. He was now cured of all that, though he still had some weakness for Netaji and was less antagonistic towards Gandhiji. He was attracted to Sarat Bose, though not to his party. He held some hope in the idea of 'Sovereign Bengal' touted by Suhrawardy and Sarat Bose, but had suspicions in this respect. He had heard what Shyamaprasad Mukherjee had had to say; the problem was highlighted thence. Shyamaprasad had expressed his doubts about it to Gandhiji. Sovereign Bengal seemed like another trick invented by the British. One wondered whether the people who were its propagators knew what it entailed, or had simply swallowed the bait. Gora did not harbour any sympathy towards Shyamaprasad, though it was he who had said that there was something fishy about the idea of Sovereign Bengal.

Biju, Satu, and Gora, three friends, came from three different families, mainly belonging to the middle class, though somewhat disparate. Biju was amongst the few really rich in the city who had landed property in the Barh region to the south of Bengal, and was reputed to have a huge income and all kinds of businesses as well. Gora's father had a respectable income at one time; perhaps its source was the jute mills, but whatever real business the family had had came to an end two or three generations ago. Whatever the reason, whether owing to the lack of animal farming pastures or the absence of agricultural land, the family was drawn to industries a few generations ago. It was Gora's grandfather who had first built a regular two-storey brick building in place of an ordinary thatched-roofed ancestral home. Gora's elder brother bought a house along with half a portion of a big garden, the land of a poor Brahmin neighbour, and many more such. He stayed in one of the jute mill officer's quarters, was more or less a sahib, and had married but was without children. The people in the neighbourhood gossiped that Gora would become the heir to all his fortune. In addition, there was another rumour that since Gurudas—Gora's elder brother—maintained good relations with his in-laws, and because these relations visited him often, it was likely that whatever he had in cash, movable and immovable property would go to his brother-in-law's children. When one mentioned this likelihood to Gora, he would pronounce, with nose in the air, 'Gora Ghosh does not hanker after other's wealth. Why only Gurudas? Haren Ghosh too can give away his land and property to whoever he chooses. I do not want anything. As they say in English, "I am grateful to my father that he gave me a chance to educate myself in the other way. Now I can find my way and earn my bread. That is enough."'

Gora was the first descendent of his family who didn't go in for a job in the jute mills. He had an MA in Bengali, and because he didn't do well in his exams, he was thinking of taking up English Studies. He had at present three tuitions to depend upon. Of course, he could do more tutoring, but did not wish to. He was addicted to bidis, and at times smoked cigarettes and loved to haunt tea shops. Nevertheless, both Biju and Satu knew that Gora's father was very fond of his son. Gora's mother passed away many years ago. His two elder sisters were married and lived in Naihati. A middle-aged woman, belonging to a poor relative, cooked and took care of their entire household. She knew that Gora's father would refuse to take his meal both at noon and at night unless Gora was back home, and also that he was mentally at rest only if Gora sent a message beforehand. One could not fathom from his outside appearance how much eagerness and anxiety he constantly harboured regarding his son. Of course, Gora too doted on his father, who was now past seventy-five years of age. He had been fit for work till he reached seventy, but the company refused to let him retire. The father and son were like friends; they sat together and shared a laugh and gossiped. Haru Ghosh was the living example of how far the liberalism of a company servant could go. It was all apparent while talking and joking with Gora, although all this may not have seemed proper to the aforementioned gentlemen of the locality.

Biju belonged to a rich family, but was extremely courteous, hard-working, and educated, and much loved by his father for being first born. Yet, Biju was not the spoilt son of a rich parent and did not put on any airs. Though he had a lot of respect for his father, he could not always follow his dictate. Sachindra Mitra was extremely communal, a feudal in temperament, and along with this, the target of the provincials. He hardly conversed with Satu and Gora, his son's friends, and exchanged a few words with Biju only when absolutely necessary. He would rather tell his wife any complaint he might have against his son. But that was also the source of his weakness. Although Biju's mother was a conservative lady, she thought Biju could do no wrong. And if she had had any qualms, neither Satu nor Gora could have had any access to the household. She did not always follow all the rules her husband made regarding Biju. In fact, Sachindra Mitra's feudal temperament had to take a retreat when confronted by her. Biju had a brother and a sister younger to him. His uncles, both the older and the younger ones, had a share in their landed estate in the Barh region. Next to them lay the great estate of the Mittirs with their large houses.

Satu belonged to a Chatterjee family of declining fortunes in the same town. I say declining because at one time they were regarded as landholders or zemindars. This was not hard to guess from the ruins of the Chatterjees' grand old building and the scorched earth lying next to the Ganges river bed. Many such falling houses belonging to the one-time rural rich could be found in the adjoining villages. People would not have worried their heads about the history of the family, had Raja Ram Mohan not come from such a family. It's redundant, therefore, to trace the rise and fall of the Chatterjee dynasty. Nothing remained of the family's large estates, huge income, wealth, and elegance. Now the vagabonds have taken shelter in whatever existed of the ancient ruins. Some of them, however, had made their dwellings in the best way they could. In the neighbourhood, some had even raised one or two-storey houses, found jobs, started small businesses, and thus, in these minor ways, the later generation of the Chatterjees had tried to preserve their identity like any other ordinary people in the region. Satu was the child of such a family. His father had died long ago. He had four brothers and two sisters, one elder to him, the other younger. The brothers all worked, were married, and lived separately. His didi got married when his father was still alive. They somehow together were able to give the younger sister away in marriage. Of course, Satu hardly played a role in all this. He continued to live under the guardianship of his widowed mother and an elder brother, though never a very obedient boy. Always a bit footloose and fancy-free, he somehow managed to pass his matriculation. Satu could never keep the promises he made or or remain subservient to his elder brother, though he was in his keep. Therefore, his independent stance came to be taken as a sign of waywardness. Neglect and lack of love were inevitably his lot. But the care and affection of an anxious mother protected him in this world. Satu was sympathetic towards his mother. He went ahead with his life, making sure that his mother was kept safe and sound the remaining years of her life. There was nothing desperate or aggressive about this. He was after all the *nawalkishore*, the eternal youth of the Vaishnav poetry. He had come to know of love in his early years, had always regarded studies as a dull affair, and was completely drawn to the art of poetry. His mind and attitude was romantic, and he was hard-working, but had done what many in the neighbourhood found reprehensible. Pratima, a girl of a *kayet* (inferior caste) family, became his mistress. The event took place three years ago, an event considered even more devilishly daring when Satu went and married her. Pratima's family did not approve and even went to the court to oppose the liaison. But Pratima had already crossed the age of sixteen (age of consent), therefore, neither the law nor the police could do anything about it. Now Satu was the father of a son; he had a small job in a semi-toolshed built by the Americans as a part of a large factory during the war years.

Therefore, at a first glance, there existed the vast discrepancy between the three friends in their family background, education, work experience, etc. Despite all this, and differences notwithstanding, the three were friends. But what was the relationship between Gora and Sudhaboudi? It was unclear to both Satu and Biju. Though that's not quite correct. Gora started to blush the minute Sudhaboudi's name was mentioned. He had nothing to hide from his friends, but felt embarrassed ever so slightly, and inhibited. And amidst all the hesitation, a flash of joy sent light waves through his frame.

Almost thirty years of age, Sudhaboudi was older than Gora. Satu and Biju, both had a great deal of respect for her. And Gora? Did he too feel the same way about her? One was used to hearing him shower praise on her, at times indeed forgetting himself, overwhelmed as he would be, talking about her, especially when he would recall, 'I have no way to stop her if she makes up her mind that I have to have dinner before I come away from her place, and stay back to have dinner. I must....But I feel sorry about her at times. One cannot imagine the emptiness in her life seeing her from the outside. What does she have—money, property? Although I know that her son is the most precious thing in her life, and Prakashda—it's amazing that a girl like her should have a husband like Prakashda! Prakashda is mad, an imbecile, gentle no doubt, but who knows whether he deserves to be a husband.' Gora often forgot propriety and referred to Sudhaboudi as she or her, and only reverted back to Sudhaboudi when Satu or Biju mentioned her as such. Some days, he even started calling her by her name 'Sudha', so forgetful he tended to be, then retreated shame-faced, realizing his blunder. Once he went so far as to declare to both Satu and Biju that if anyone (in the whole town) came and stood in the way of his getting to see her, he would overcome all barriers to reach her place. But did he not understand then that he was supposed to go to her house to teach Sudhaboudi's seven-year-old son and not just to see her? He would be there twice a week even two years ago; the boy was five then. The number of visits increased steadily, and he went there everyday now. Did people in the region think badly of him for this? He asked his friends, looking at both with enquiring eyes. But the answer lay within himself.

And what did Biju say to all this? His reply was straightforward, 'Why should I think badly of you? Are the people who are speaking bad of Sudhaboudi, and dragging your name in dirt, all good people? Don't know what kind of person Prakashda is, a mad man or an imbecile, but if Sudhaboudi had not been there, we would have found him on the streets or in the station, begging. I don't care what people say. I don't believe a word of it. What do you say, Satu?'

'I think the same way,' Satu's stand was even more clear. And perhaps carried a few hints as well. He said, 'And what is wrong if Sudhaboudi trusts Gora? Don't we know what kind of people Sukumarda and his sons are? Isn't it necessary for Sudhaboudi to have a trusted friend or a relative? And if that person happens to be Gora, how does that matter? Gora himself has told us that Sudhaboudi can't trust her own family. Her brothers had married their sister off to someone like Prakashda knowingly. Sudhaboudi thinks it was some kind of conspiracy, else how could they have given their beautiful sister away to a person like Prakashda? That's why

Sudhaboudi has almost stopped inviting her family to her home. That means that she has found out what their real intentions are. In the event, if Gora, heeding to all the gossip, stops going to Sudhaboudi's house, I, myself, will call him a coward before others do.'

Gora was full of gratitude after listening to Biju and Satu, and that feeling of gratitude was but another expression of the strength he imbibed from their friendship. Satu and Biju had noticed that Gora wanted to say much more about himself, but could not as something came in the way of his being totally frank, and because he could not open his heart, no matter how much he tried. He suffered and was uncomfortable. There was a manifestation of regret and apology in his shy and troubled smile. Perhaps, that was natural. One could not stretch oneself beyond a point. Perhaps, if one crossed the limits of legitimacy, one would have insulted Sudhaboudi. Neither Satu nor Biju could dream of making such a demand of Gora. They were, after all, sensitive. Nevertheless, it seemed that an enigma at times roused their extreme curiosity. Satu ruminated to himself:

'O light, don't penetrate deep into the shadows,/O insightful, sometimes even the dark has reason/Have not you seen this truth within you?/Hasn't the dark fortnight roused questions that resides beyond light?'

'No, don't open your packet now,' Gora clamped his palm over Satu's. 'Let us finish mine first, and yes, she has asked us to come over to her place this evening. Manik will not be taking his lessons for the next seven days.'

Satu puckered his brows and looked at Biju as if surprised, likewise Biju. Satu turned to Gora, 'Has Sudhaboudi asked us to come?'

'Yes,' Gora laughed, bringing out a cigarette and offering it to Satu. He took one himself and put the packet back into his pocket. 'She told me, "Bring your friends Satu and Biju to my place in the evening. I have sweets for you all today."' Gora lit up a cigarette and held the burning match towards Biju, who gave his cigarette a pull, while Satu leaned over to light up his, rubbing off the burning matchstick against the parapet. He smiled, 'Honestly, no third man! Actually she would've asked us to come tomorrow, that is August 15, but her sister-in-law is due to arrive, a sister-in-law nobody cares for. I'll perhaps go and see her for a short while.' Satu lit up another cigarette. 'I haven't visited Sudhaboudi for over three years. Does not matter; will be tasting the sweets she makes after a long time.'

'But she's really fond of Pratima,' Gora smiled. 'You'll get to hear all about it when you go.'

Just at the moment, Kanchana appeared on the terrace with three cups of hot tea. She came pressing her lips tightly, as if like an acrobat in a circus, carefully tiptoeing her way. Her fair face was red, minute drops of perspiration covered her visage. Gora took a leap and came face to face with her, then withdrawing somewhat, and biting his tongue like Goddess Kali, said, 'Gosh, I'd quite forgotten! Why did you have to come yourself carrying these?' He took the cups of tea carefully from her hands.

Biju and Satu advanced towards Gora, who lifted a cup and saucer and gave it to Satu, then took the other one from Kanchana. Biju, of course, lifted his cup directly from Kanchana's hands. Kanchana heaved a sigh of relief.

'Who can I ask to bring them here? You have to just go and order. I thought of asking Lokkhi to take them, but Gupida told me that Dada had forbidden all belonging to the household to come up to the terrace. Did you?'

'Yes, I have. Can't you see I am smoking?' Biju shook his head. 'I had kept the door open for Gora, and talked to Gupida about his coming. But how would I know you'd be bringing our tea?'

Kanchana pointed to Gora, 'Tell him what all you wish to say. Gorada went into the inner rooms as soon as he arrived. Ma knows that I don't like Basanti to do my hair. I simply don't care for it. But even so, Basanti is here to tie up Ma's hair. Gora had appeared there and asked whether you were at the terrace, whether you had been given tea. I said "no", and immediately Gora ordered me to take three cups of tea up to the terrace. Thank goodness, Ma's in a good mood, else she would've thrown a fit.'

'That's enough! Mashima herself asked me, "Gora, what is going to be the fate of the Khulna district?"' Gora laughed and glanced at Biju. 'I said, "Rest assured, Khulna will remain firmly inside India."' Biju and Satu exchanged looks. The cigarette dangling from the fingers of Biju's right hand was sending up curls of smoke. He sipped the tea and said, 'One cannot contradict Radcliff's secret message, can one?'

Satu now shook in glee, the hot tea spilling all over his trembling hands. Kanchana, her other name being Moni, also broke into peals of laughter. She was sixteen years old, identical to Biju in looks, almost as tall, one could say, rather ungainly, but because a woman, her height added to her attractiveness. She was preparing to sit for her matriculation during that year, and had been working at it since the year before. But the riots had spoilt all that.

Gora stuck his nose up in the air, 'Dears! Sir Cyril Radcliffe hasn't whispered into the ears, has he?' His moustache was now stiff and sharp as the blades of the sword. 'Mansur Mallik, the Muslim League leader of Calcutta, gave me the news a short while ago and also said, "Better get to hear this—the rich Hindu zemindars of the Khulna district are raising a few crores of rupees." "But for whom is all the money raised?" I asked Mallik Sahib. He laughed and patted my back and said, "That I cannot tell you, but you can ask Comrade Tarakbabu or at the least Surenbabu about it. Do you know that Khulna is the only district out of the entire Presidency region that is being considered for being handed over to East Pakistan? Now, not even twenty-four hours remain for the country's independence—to arrive at this decision is like gambling with fate. And I don't think it can lead to anything good. I am only praying to Allah that Gandhiji does not leave Calcutta. I don't worry my head over which district falls into whose hands. I worry about communal violence, and know that there will be peace if Gandhiji is around. Calcutta is not yet free of the incidents of riot. The newspapers have reported a few minor incidents. All this will come to a stop if Gandhiji stayed back. Even Khulna won't create a problem."' He gave a sip. 'Now it is up to you whether to believe all of this or not.'

All of a sudden, neither Biju nor Satu could utter a word. Whatever smile there was now vanished from their faces. They turned serious and dark. Likewise, Kanchana's. They were all taken aback at Gora's mention of the name of Mansur Mallik Sahib, a highly respected gentleman of the neighbourhood, whose words were hard not to believe. It was said that his grandfather Mohammad Rasul Mallik had arrived at the Calcutta port from Uttar Pradesh as a chieftain. He had joined the jute mills along with his band of workers after some misunderstanding with the port authorities. Everyone knew him as Rasul Sardar, but it wasn't that he was someone like a headman of jute mills. First of all, he was extraordinarily good-looking, and besides being polite and religious, was grave and imposing in demeanour. The workers had never heard him utter a harsh word; he never raised his hands on anyone and always addressed them as his sons, a rare phenomenon among the headmen of jute mills. All of them, the Khalifas or the big bosses, belied whatever sense of respect and honour the description conveyed. People understood Mastan or Khalifa to imply someone who was quick-tempered, foul-mouthed, rowdy, given to brawling, murderous, secretive, etc.

No worker under Rasul Sardar had ever been disobedient, and they also never had to appear before the police for any conflict or inner fighting that might have taken place among themselves, in which case Mohammad Rasul Sardar was always the final judge and they willingly accepted his verdict. The sardar too never extorted money from the workers, which most of his kind did. First of all, the sardars, all of them, were entitled to something 'extra', something all the bosses demanded. Rasul Sardar accepted whatever came his way—from two paisa to, at the most, six annas per head *nazrana* or something extra like that. All the workers under him—be they Hindus or Muslims—were happy with him, had both fear and respect for him, and they never cheated him at work.

Handsome Mohammad Rasul Mallik was highly respected even by the British officers of the company. He had a good reputation among the middle-class Bengali bhadraloks as well. Hardly anyone belonging to the Bengali Hindu neighbourhood objected or complained when he built his own home in a thoroughly Bengali Hindu colony. Rather, everyone gazed in admiration at the tall, fair, handsome man with a mehendi-tinted beard, wearing one of those long, flowing, white kalidar panjabi and white pyjamas, and a white delicately embroidered skull cap while promenading in the area.

His Hindi was weak; he had admitted his only son Mohammad Gulam Rasul Mallik straightway in a Bengali high school, after an early education in a madrasa, followed by a period of tutoring at the hands of a Bengali teacher at home. Rasul Sardar had from thence changed the course of his life, without making him a Hindu, giving his son a good education and making him a well-educated Muslim instead. And perhaps that was what was most needed. Mohammad Gulam studied along with Hindu Bengali youths, and passed out from Hooghly College with a BA pass after qualifying for his matriculation. His only son Mansur Mallik too studied along with other Bengali youths. His father had not lived long. He could not achieve what his father wanted to in life unlike Mansur. He took up law in Calcutta University, passing out with a BA from Hooghly College. He had been a supporter of Fazlul Huq ever since and a member of the League when Fazlul Huq became one. But somehow, he could never strike up a good relationship with either Nazimuddin or Suhrawardy.

Mansur Mallik was initially a member of the Congress Party. He joined the Muslim League after a brief stint with Krishak Praja Party (Fazlul Huq's party). Alipore Judge's Court was his place of work. He never lived in Calcutta, but in a place twenty miles to the north where the family home was, and from there he commuted to work daily. He did not spend the night in Calcutta unless urgently required. Nevertheless, duty beckoned him to Calcutta today. It just so happened that he was always present where all the trouble took place. To put on record, last year, he was perhaps the only Muslim person by the name of Mansur Mallik, the grandson of a headsman of a jute mill, an emigrant from UP and a Bengali by adoption, who declared in a August 14 meeting of the Muslims that Nazimuddin has in fact lied. 'You must not forget that Quaid Azam Jinnah has not been able to accept a single word of the new president of the Congress Party (Nehru). I think Jawaharlalji, the new Congress president, has not said the right thing. The Congress Party had agreed upon the Cabinet Mission plan, yet he has gone on to say that the parliament of the sovereign republic is not bound to adhere to the dictates of the Congress Party. Although we were all so elated, when, within a week, both the Congress and the Muslim League together agreed upon the May 16 Cabinet Mission plan. And just imagine when Jawaharlalji said something like this on July 10, Jinnah Sahib was furious because he knew that the Cabinet Mission, the Governor General, and the British rulers were having a good laugh witnessing all the fiasco. Jinnah Sahib called for Direct Action against the British Rule, and what did Nazimuddin Sahib go and do? He was lying when he said that Jinnah's call for Direct Action was not against the British but the Hindus. As a Muslim I am ashamed to admit to you that Nazimuddin Sahib told an absolute lie. And above all, this Suhrawardy has declared the day after tomorrow to be a holiday. They are both playing with fire. I am entreating you, don't give the Hindu–Muslim gangsters any opportunity to come to blows on the day after tomorrow that might usher in the final Day of Judgement (*keyamat*). You are all Muslims; if you wish to participate in direct action and not go to the factory tomorrow, so be it. But don't stop the Hindus. We will lay down our lives, but won't allow unnecessary fight between the Hindus and the Muslims.'

Mansur Sahib hadn't lied about Jawaharlal. There was much that was not clear in the matter. Mansur Mallik did not address only one meeting in the industrial area; he had gone around different places last year and had delivered the same talk. Jinnah's call for direct action coming soon after Jawaharlal's pronouncement was enough to set Calcutta ablaze. There was no mention of this inside the Congress Party last year. The communists did not oppose it either. But, of course, although Mansur Mallik made Jawaharlal responsible for the mess, his real target was Nazimuddin's treacherous behaviour.

The riots had taken place in Calcutta on August 16 last year, but its consequences had dragged on till this year. It had also spread far and wide, but somehow this industrial hub had escaped it all and communal harmony still obtained in the region. There was uninterrupted peace there then as now. The rioteers had tried to penetrate the industrial sector with all their might, but no community—neither Hindus nor the Muslims—allowed them to do that. And all this was possible because of a person like Mansur Mallik Sahib. The authorities of the jute mill (for interest of their own) had also wholeheartedly wished for the riots to take place, but their hopes remained unfulfilled. Many say that Mansur Sahib is a clever man. He knows that the Hindus in the industrial region far outnumber the Muslims, and that in the event of a riot, it would be Muslims who would get killed, and their property looted. That was why, keeping the fate of the Muslims in mind, he had taken leave of his law court, was hobnobbing with the communists, and propagating against communal riots. But it is also true that people from the Congress Party and not just the communists were present at every meeting he addressed. There is one class of people in the world who have existed historically. They remain today and will remain in the future, people who can always be bought over.

Tea and cigarettes were consumed in silence while light still flickered from the embers of the leftover stubs. Mallikbari (the house of the Malliks) was in the area where Gora lived. He knew all the people there as he was also known to them. Gora let out a puff of smoke. 'Mallik Sahib was getting down from a cycle rickshaw in front of his house, returning from Calcutta,' he interjected. 'I had already noticed that quite a few local Muslims had gathered on the raised terrace in front of the building. Everybody knew that Mansur Sahib had declared he would not desert his ancestral lodgings and take off elsewhere, that he, like his father and his grandfather, would breathe his last here. The local Muslims were all eagerly waiting for him when, getting down from the rickshaw, he called me to himself. I could see he was slightly distraught. He said, "I will not speak of this to anyone. The people will get to hear of it from the radio rather than hearing me. They say this. The over-enthusiastic members of the League nowadays taunt me and say nasty things about me, say I am a two-faced lackey, a double dealer. I want Pakistan and, at the same time, call Nazimuddin and Suhrawardy names and agitate against communal violence. It were better I killed a Hindu instead; it would have been a really good act." Gandhiji had on his way to Sodepore from Patna declared, "The whole of India or Bharat is my country!" A few Muslims have written insinuatingly about this in some papers. If only they had understood what Gandhi actually meant (what he had in heart when he uttered these words). I myself today feel like declaring that all of Bharat is my country. Actually, what did he mean? No matter what be the reason for the British to go and divide the country, I'll go everywhere, stay put in every place. Leave all this, Gora. I have told you so many things today. Everybody is giving me looks. Yes, I did want Pakistan and am now striving to get it. But there is no joy in all this. My heart is about to burst. Why? I don't have any idea what's happening in the country ... ' saying this, he walked away.

'But Gorada, what is the harm if Khulna is taken out of the Presidency division and put inside West Bengal?' Kanchana said with a demanding voice. Taking a last pull, Satu rubbed the stub of his fag against the parapet. 'See dear, when the country is being divided according to the ratio of population, the question of Presidency division does not arise.'

'If that were the case, Murshidabad should have been included in East Pakistan,' Biju interjected, throwing away the remains of the cigarette at the corner of the terrace. 'The way the Boundary Commission have done their work is very complicated. There are many places which are dominantly Hindu, where the Muslim population is also substantial and those have remained within West Bengal.'

Satu shook his head, 'Yes, Calcutta, 24 Parganas, Darjeeling, Jalpaiguri have all been kept inside West Bengal, though some problems regarding Jalpaiguri remain. But let me ask again, what about Maldah or Nadia? The Pathan soldiers have committed atrocities in Dinajpur even eight days ago. Why? Was it just like that? Hard to believe. Something must have happened—the Pathans were deliberately provoked. You say that Murshidabad ought to have been included in East Pakistan. How did this idea occur to you when the Boundary Commission exists? Is it because Murshidabad is very much the decision of the Boundary Commission?'

'Mind you, Radcliffe can at any moment make a contrary declaration. There are many who have problems and doubts about the fate of Murshidabad. Some say there was a mistake in transcription, others that the Boundary Commission had resorted to a temporary bluff following Radcliffe's dictate. You are not paying attention to Mansur Sahib's devastating statement about the rich Hindu landlords of Khulna raising a few crores of rupees. For whom? Mallik Sahib cannot talk openly about this. It's dangerous to do that. Don't I want to know what Jawaharlal and Patel are talking about? Do they know what all are happening or don't they? Is it only Gandhi who realizes what we will be faced with if we accept the decision of the British to divide the country? Is all this still not clear? Gandhiji has not been able to accept with full heart the division of the country till today. Now the money game has begun, though not a word of this is mentioned in the media or uttered by the leaders. Do you think that only the zemindars of Khulna are stashed with money and not the non-Bengali Muslims of Calcutta? One Ispahani can buy off a considerable portion of West Bengal. I don't like all this, don't like a thing. I am going to Beliaghata, today, now!'

'Satu-u-u,' Biju rested an arm on Satu's shoulders.

Was Satu trying to hide his tears? His eyes had become somewhat red! He looked as if he was in pain, yet his head shook in agitation. 'I don't feel like reading the newspapers. I don't want to hear what all the leaders have to say, since India is becoming independent at such a cost! If I wish to be happy, then it is enough to go to Beliaghata and stand in front of that one person who I have never thus far laid my eyes on. I think he came to Naihati for a short while, on his way to Assam some eight or nine years ago. It had already become late by the time I got to know about it. Nevertheless, I rushed only to find his saloon had left.'

'Look, Satu. It's no use being sentimental,' Gora took out a cigarette.

Satu's voice rang loudly in protest. 'Sentimental? How can you say that of me after hearing what Mallik Sahib had to say? Are you going to expound the two-nation theory to me? Or teach me to find solace in the idea of a sovereign Bengal? Why did Gandhiji reject Saratbabu's proposal even if one were to ignore Shyamaprosad's suspicions? Today nobody is talking about the money game behind the Boundary Commission's decision. As if it isn't there. But remember, Nawabzada Liaquat Ali himself had rushed to Calcutta with a sack full of currency notes before the proposal for the division of the country was placed before the previous state assembly. This news was not printed either in *Ananda Bazar* or *Amrita Bazar,* but was splashed in the Muslim League run English daily. And you call me sentimental? The British will try to divide the country because that is their sweet will. Radcliffe heads the Boundary Commission. And none of us have a clue about the secret game of money laundering that is taking place. What all is happening? What all are we accepting without a murmur?'

'Listen Satuda, know why I had brought up the topic of Khulna?' Kanchana laughed and wiped the perspiration off her face with the edge of her green saree. 'Oh dear, you speak so gravely about all kinds of things that I am afraid to mention anything. Actually, Asasuni in Khulna is my uncle's place. How will I visit my maternal uncle's home if it becomes Pakistan?'

Biju puckered his brows, but Gora burst into laughter, 'Moni, you have said something close to your heart, I must say,' he added.

'Really!' Satu smiled. 'Moni's maternal uncle's home will disappear if one gets to hear tomorrow that it is being included in Pakistan. No? Dear Moni, know how many maternal uncles' home, or one's own homes are about to disappear? But don't take a fright. I am neither angry nor being quarrelsome. I want to enjoy myself, really do! Only at times I feel a stab of pain somewhere in my heart, I don't know why. Especially after listening to Mallik Sahib....But let that be...Come Moni, let's sing that song. You begin.

Dhana Dhyanya —

The last rays of the sun on top of the rich, colour-drenched foliage in the western sky were smothering away whatever remained of the gloom. A bright red sun was sinking in all its glory. The orange-tinted river appeared as if made of waves of blood. A spurt of red was also on the faces of people on the terrace. Kanchana laughed, her eyes and face suffused with bashfulness. She wiped her face again with the end of her saree. Then she took up the song in her young but melodious voice:

Dhana Dhyanya Pushpe Bhara
Amader e Basundhara
Tahar Majhe Achhe Desh Ek
Sakal Desher Sera
Fields of golden grain
Meadows of fragrant flowers/
The delights of our earth
Nestled within which is a land
above all measure

Satu now added his voice to Kanchana's, then Biju joined in. And last of all, Gora.

Nobody made any mistake in the melody. Only Gora's heavy baritone voice sounded a bit cracked. The boys and girls on the neighbouring terrace looked at them and listened to their song. The four kept on singing:

Swapna Diye Tairi Se Desh
Smriti Diye Ghera
Emon Deshti Kothay Khuje
Pabe Nako Tumi
Sakal Desher Rani Se Je
Amar Janmabhumi
Se Je Amar Janmabhumi
Created from dreams
Anchored by memory
Nowhere can you find
A land
That is the Queen of this earth
This land of my birth
The hallowed land of my birth

She stood on top of the stairs as if a bright flame emitting radiance all about her. Sudhaboudi was wearing a finely textured, handwoven white cotton saree with a dark blue border—so dark that it could easily be mistaken for a black border wrapped around her. She wore a black blouse with puffed-up sleeves under a rather ordinary saree. How tall was she? 5 and ½ feet? Perhaps, an inch or two less. Her fair arms seemed to throw off brightness from underneath the saree cover, as did too the diamond nose ring from her finely pointed nose. A red dot on her forehead, the veil slipping down her back, revealing a huge bun. Her eyes were not large, but slanted upwards, making them appear big. But without any kohl. Yet, the dense blackness of her orbs sent off sharp glances. Thinly arched brows on a fairly wide forehead. There was a line of red sindur on her hair parting. Her lips were like those of the stone-sculpted temple nymphs, red with betel nut juice. There were a few gold bangles and conch shell armlets around her arms, a fine gold chain around her neck, and the two fair feet were painted red. The attractiveness of her taut, finely shaped body seemed to strike one again and again. Sudhaboudi was standing in front of the stairs, laughing at the sight of the three friends, their lips painted red in betel nut juice, but pairs of shiny white teeth showing from between them. She shook her head and called them in, 'Come in. All of you are panting so! Have you come running?' There was so much joy and camaraderie in her voice!

'Yes,' said Gora, his one foot inside the threshold. Looking back, he called out to the other two, 'Come on in.'

Sudhaboudi was by then walking into the right side of the interior courtyard, her back to them. She ought to have been named Sugata, such a beautiful gait she had! Satu thought. Although he had the same idea about Pratima too, which soon enough came to his mind. It was useless to compare both. Sudhaboudi was extraordinarily good-looking and a rich housewife; in comparison, Pratima was the wife of poverty-stricken Satu. No matter how fair she was, Pratima's bright looks were faded, worn away by soot from the open oven, the grind of domestic work, and the heat and dust of the environment in which she lived. She tried to somehow maintain whatever grace she had, and kept herself neat and tidy, but the dark rings under her eyes never seemed to disappear. That was also because she was not given the care due to her after childbirth. No nose ring adorned her nose. Nevertheless, despite all the deprivation, her good health continued to attract people, and no sign of gloom ever shadowed her endearing smile.

Crossing the courtyard, Sudhaboudi entered a room lit up by electric lights. One could see a veiled woman (married) amidst the half shadows inside the room to the right. There was no wind in the air, yet one could feel a mild breeze wafting into the room filled with fragrance. It was emanating from Sudhaboudi's frame. The blue-bordered saree cover had slipped off her hair bun. Were they a garland of flowers—*bakul* or *jui*—tied around the bun? Sraban was the month of those flowers. It was but natural that Sudhaboudi should have them on her. The doors of the room to the left of the room into which she entered was open, a light switched on inside. Sudhaboudi gave Gora a sidelong glance ere she entered the room and said, 'Bring your friends in. See what your student is up to.'

'Come along,' Gora told Satu and Biju, beckoning them inside.

There was an egg-shaped marble table on a polished, red cemented floor, surrounded by some brightly polished, unpadded chairs with handles. Manik was Sudhaboudi's seven-year-old son, resembling the mother, wearing half-pants and blue half-sleeved shirt. He was busy making a chain out of white-, green-, and earth-coloured paper, used for making kites. He was trying but couldn't. All the effort like cutting the paper and preparing the glue were done by a middle-aged woman dressed in widow's robes. There were two national flags mounted on iron poles resting on one corner of the wall. Manik looked up at Satu and Biju, glanced at Gora, and said, 'How is it that you are here? Ma says I have seven days' holidays from today!'

'Holidays, of course,' Sudhaboudi smiled, gazing at her son. 'The heavens seem to fall if you are asked to sit and study.' Sudhaboudi turned to the three friends and said, 'You all sit. I can't be polite and address you formally; haven't all these years either. Besides, you are so much younger to me!'

The three stared at each other, a smile of surprise on their faces, and they roared in laughter.

'Can't remember you ever addressing me formally as *apni* or responding ceremonially as *agye*,' said Biju, a flicker of amusement in his dark large eyes. Satu took his packet of Capstan from out of his trouser pocket, looked at Sudhaboudi, and said, 'I haven't visited in the last three years, but I remember you always addressing me as *tumi* (you).'

'But you've become a father in the three years we haven't met. You are now a real man; you might take offense if I don't address you formally!'

The three again looked at each other and roared in laughter.

Satu found that Sudhaboudi was looking intently at him, as if deeply scrutinizing him. He felt slightly embarrassed, 'What's this about becoming a proper man! Ain't I the same Satu?'

'Lies,' Sudhaboudi now looked at Gora. 'A Brahmin's son, you go and bring a fully grown *kayet* girl into your house, marry her, and then make a child with her,' she hardly finished saying than her face became a bright red.

Biju laughed, 'Sudhaboudi is correct. Are you that same Satu? Got married, produced a son, and, above all this, you have a moustache that falls on your mouth like those of the unshaven Bihari jute-mill workers, which you ever so often twirl with your fingers.'

'Ugh, so ugly,' Sudhaboudi screwed her nose as if in disgust. The diamond on it was throwing off sparks. 'Doesn't Pratima complain? If it had been me, I would have trimmed it with scissors. And see how someone is sporting a moustache like those great Englishmen one comes across in book illustrations! Just because I don't possess a razor! Your Prakashda can't be bothered with such things! The barber comes and trims his beard, else I would have done it myself—shaved them off clean one day.'

Satu and Biju gave a good laugh. 'I understand that the lifespan of my moustache can't be long….' Gora said, smiling and rolling his moustache, looking stupid.

'Sit sit, why keep standing?' Sudhaboudi turned to Manik. 'Manik dear, take all these things and go and sit in your room or the courtyard. Sukodidi, please gather all these carefully and take them away. I'm going to feed Manik's master and uncles with tea and snacks here.'

Sukodidi had already covered her head. She now collected the strewn colourful papers and the paper chain with her left hand and put them into the wicker basket along with a pair of scissors. Manik held out his arms and took the basket, saying, 'Sukomashi, you bring the pot of glue.'

One could hardly see Sukomashi's veiled face. She nodded her head in assent and went out of the room. Satu was gazing at the wall. Just one picture on it—Subhash Bose's portrait, a rather big one framed in glass. A door and two windows on the eastern side of the room were open. One could detect a verandah, dark with no lights on, and next to it a garden with a lot of foliage. A pond surrounded by a wall bordering it. There were roads on either side of the building. The view of the house was familiar to all in the neighbourhood. Sukumar Mukherjee occupied a large portion of the western and southern parts of the building. Sukumar happened to be Prakash's elder brother. There was eighteen or nineteen years' difference between the two. In between were two or three sisters. Where was Prakashda? Satu was curious. At times, one could find him roaming aimlessly in the streets; he did not do that anymore. He was not insane; there was nothing abnormal about him, only he wore a vacant look in his eyes. The words he uttered were rather indistinct that was when he attempted to speak; which was rare. His face was expressionless. One could not fathom whether he felt any emotion, be they one of joy, sorrow, laughter, or tears. His body was well-built, nothing odd or deformed about it. He had a good health. A quiet man, he had to be held to make him sit down, and food served when eating. There was something quite not right with him, of this one had no doubt. Really, why did Sudhaboudi's father or brothers marry her, a beautiful girl, to such a person? One cannot but be suspicious about this. And what was the relationship between the husband and wife? Did Sudhaboudi love her husband? Or did she just pity him like one does a pet animal? It was not difficult to fathom that she had a rather deep friendship with Gora.

'Delighted with the pack of cigarettes we all are, and that also so sudden—' Biju took his packet of Capstan from out of his panjabi pocket. 'It is as yet unopened and so is Satu's,' he said. 'Gora allowed us to smoke his.'

Sudhaboudi now drew a chair and settled near them. The texture of her white saree was fine as milky white *garad* silk. The golden hue of her fair skin radiated from underneath the saree and the black puff-sleeved blouse. Her frame, eyes, face, and her smile were all redolent with a sense of joy. 'What can I give you, as a present on our independence day, tell me? Thought I'd give you a packet of cigarette each. Manik's master uncle said I could give a magnum-sized Capstan. Master uncle himself helped to buy those. Then I thought, who after all do I have, save you two young brothers-in-law who I care for? That's why I thought, let me feed you sweets today. Tomorrow my sister-in-law will arrive. She is widowed and lives in Baichi. Being extremely poor, and with three grown-up daughters and two sons, she has no landed property of any description. Who knows why the poor dear was married off to an old man knowingly? And now that the country will become independent, it does not mean her daughters can be married off just like that. All kinds of expenses, including dowry, have to be taken care of.' Sudha came to a stop, her face turning grim. Then, she suddenly broke into a smile, 'But leave all that. And tell me, why did you come running? What was the reason for the hurry?'

'Yes, we are indeed in a desperate hurry,' Gora gave Satu and Biju a hurried look. 'Tell Hira to quickly bring the sweets. We, I mean Satu has decided that he will take the first train to Calcutta.'

'Calcutta? At this evening hour. But why?' Sudhaboudi looked at Satu, raising her brows.

Satu laughed, 'Want to go to Beliaghata Hyderi Mansion only to see Gandhiji, this once. Will get back soon after.'

'You are being stupid,' although Sudhaboudi was laughing, there was a tone of reprimand in her voice. 'The evening has just begun. The day has become longer. Though it's almost seven, the locals normally don't run according to time. You know this better than I do. Besides, there is curfew in Calcutta from ten or eleven at night. How will you get to Sealdah if it gets late? It were better that you go tomorrow morning; you will be able to have his darshan. Don't I feel like going? I have never had the chance to see him.'

Gora shook his head, 'How'll you go leaving Manik behind?'

'Why should I leave Manik behind?' Sudhaboudi gave Gora a smile. 'If I can have darshan, why must Manik be deprived?

Why must you always think the contrary?' She glanced at Satu and Biju and laughed, 'Come on, haven't I said what's correct? Of course, I doubt I will really be able to go. I don't understand politics or such things; haven't studied that far either. The elder brother of my younger sister-in-law, he teaches at a Calcutta college. He was really good in studies, somewhat like Biju. Oh dear, Biju, why feel embarrassed? He's my younger sister-in-law's dada, Suhrid Chattopadhyay—such a big man in my eyes! He does not pontificate or have disciples, else I would have become his pupil. He's quite old now, fifty years for sure. He hasn't married nor ever will. I haven't seen anyone so devoted to Gandhi. He wears an eight-yard-long khadi dhoti and khadi shirt. And if you ask me, it is only women who can detect the good people from the bad in life and in the world! We, sisters and brothers, have learnt how to make yarn and weave cloth in the spinning wheel from Suhridda. He isn't given to bombast; he would repeat ad infinitum that a second Christ or Buddha will not appear in this world. Likewise, there can be only one Gandhi born on this earth. Suhridda can never lie. Do you know, he had once recited a story from Gandhiji's life....'

'Chhoto Boudi!' Hira called out, coming in front of the door. A married girl came in, wearing a rather neat, red-bordered saree, head covered, graceful-looking, though rather dull in colour. There were conch shell bangles and an iron bangle clasped around her wrist, a large brass tray in her hands.

'Come Hira,' Sudhaboudi stood up and said. 'You can put the tray on the table. I will serve them.'

Hira came into the room and placed the big brass tray on the table. On the tray were three middle-sized plates, filled with all kinds of sweets. Rosogollas from Haru's shop, water-filled sandesh from Chandannagar and *lengcha* from Ranaghat—such delicacies, and then three small bowls of ghugni, three metalled glasses filled with water, a brass spitbowl. Hira left, putting the tray down.

'Let's hear the story first,' Satu gazed at Sudhaboudi's face, full of eagerness. Sudhaboudi laughed, 'Well, the food has to arrive at a time like this … but since it has….'

'Never mind, its not running away,' Biju was all too eager.

Sudhaboudi again smiled and tried to pull the veil over her head rather unnecessarily. 'Although the story is not something one ought to hear in full stomach and after the satisfaction of having a good meal, it is about God appearing in the shape of a man. Gandhiji had just returned from Africa, and had forsaken wearing Western clothes and taken to covering himself with two pieces of loincloths—one to hide his shame, the other to cover his torso. Can't remember where the incident took place. Was it Gujarat or elsewhere? There was a small river, with hardly any water. Only a thin flow, with the sand bed peeping at its edges. He had gone to the riverside to wash himself. A young wife had just risen from the water completing her bath, the wet clothes managing to cover only half her body. There were people hanging about the place. Gandhiji was sure that given the opportunity, she would have covered her bosom with her hands and gone indoors.Perhaps that was what she was used to doing. What else? Gandhiji could not remain still. He took off his loincloth and let it float downstream till it neared her reach and ere she took another dip into the water. The girl, amazed to find such a big piece of cloth floating downstream, extended her hands, pulled it unto herself, and wrapped the cloth around the body. Amazed and happy, she thought perhaps it was God Himself seeing her plight … Meanwhile, Gandhiji was watching her.' Sudhaboudi's voice choked. She was smiling, but her eyes were not dancing any more. Her compassionate looks acquired another dimension as the drops of tears inside the corner of her eyes sparkled!

Nobody uttered a word. Gora and Biju were gazing intently at Sudhaboudi's face. Satu's eyes were wandering elsewhere—to the trees and the foliage enmeshed in the darkness outside. He became absent-minded, while Sudhaboudi's voice, free of constraint, continued, 'I am just an ordinary woman, that is why I can understand another woman's plight, though we don't do anything about it. When I heard Suhridda speak of him, I realized what an extraordinary person he was—I mean Gandhiji, so different from all the other leaders in the world. I had wanted to see him so much since that time. I read in the papers how people crowded to see him when he arrived at Beliaghata from Sodepur yesterday. The riots in Calcutta have simply come to a stop. What an extraordinary happening! Who is there like him? Is there really another such person?'

'There aren't any,' Satu spoke on as if in a trance; his sight was outside the building. He moved his head slowly and said, 'There is actually no one; he is the only person who does not want the country to be divided. I am going now, today itself. Want to see him just this once….'

Sudhaboudi now got up and wiped away the tears with the palm of her hand. She gave a smile, a bright and sparkling one, and soon there was a brightness all around, the orbs of her eyes radiating with glow. 'Silly! That's why I did not wish to repeat the incident to you all. It is one among the many joys of independence to go to see him and hear him speak. Freedom was on the anvil, but Calcutta was still shrouded in darkness. All that evaporated the minute he stepped into the place. But how can you travel there today? Why did you not start early if you really wanted to go? There is so much curfew, and armed policemen roaming the roads. I believe that most streets are not lighted. Give up the idea for now. Have some sweets instead!'

Biju, Gora, or Satu, none of them were wearing a watch. Biju had one, but did not wear it all the time. Gora's father had gifted his son a watch, which he put on only once in a while. As for Satu, he had none, but kept a timepiece at home. Satu took a cigarette out of the packet and pushed it between his lips. But Sudhaboudi snatched it from his lips before he could take the matchbox from out of his trouser pocket and light it. 'I see you can't think of doing anything else.' Turning to others, she said, 'He is the maddest among the lot of you, I can see.'

'Though he is a supporter of the Communist Party!' Gora laughed. 'He is a sympathizer, works for the party, and represents it as a trade union activist in his factory. And the party does not spare a thought over Gandhiji; it cannot be bothered.' Sudhaboudi placed the metalled tray with plates in front of Satu rather than the others. She smiled at Biju and Gora and said, 'So what! Can't one revere Gandhiji even if one were a communist?'

'Satu has been talking of Gandhiji continually for the last few days,' Biju looked at Satu. 'Tarakda knows everything. Satu had declared that he'll be going to see Gandhiji in front of him and Tarakda had said, "Why not? We may have many points of difference with Gandhiji, but so far as communalism goes, we are with him. It is we who wanted Jinnah and Gandhi to come together." But Tarakda cannot stand Suhrawardy.'

Sudhaboudi now put the tray with sweets in front of Biju. 'That most of us too. Of course, that aforementioned gentleman has also come to know about all this. So he had sent a messenger to Gandhiji before going to see him himself.'

'Absolutely untrustworthy, he is. All this is a pose,' Satu sounded firm. He gulped sweets in great speed and shook his head, 'Couldn't he, intelligent that he is, understand what harm he was doing to the body politic last August? Got the country up in flames trying to settle scores with Calcutta. What he is about to do now is out of fear.'

Sudhaboudi rested her arm on Gora's neck and placed the plate of sweets in front. 'Okay, that is what it was. It's not that he hasn't learnt his lesson. Now eat a bit slowly, you … '

Satu breathed in the fragrance emanating from Sudhaboudi's frame. He looked at Biju. Gora, while eating, looked at both with suspicion and frowned.

'Satu, you can't cheat me,' Sudhaboudi smiled. 'Know that you will rush to Calcutta now. Sudhaboudi has just wasted all her breath. You are different from the lot. Biju will perhaps accompany you, and I am sure the other person shan't be left behind either! But for heaven's sake, be careful what you do, and send Pratima a message before you leave. Will keep my word, won't you?'

Satu bent his head in agreement. He rapidly gulped down water from his glass. 'Of course, I will tell her before I go. You'll see us back before nightfall.' Looking at Gora, he added, 'And you must convey our news to Sudhaboudi tomorrow early morning.' Both now got up.

Sudhaboudi heaved a deep sigh, 'I know I won't be able to go and see him, no matter how much I want to. Will have to hear all about him from you all.'

Satu, Biju, and Gora, the three of them ran and entered the railway station. Satu had called out to Pratima, 'Going to Calcutta for a brief period. Will be back at night,' through his house's open window, before leaving for the station. The Down Naihati Local entered the platform, throwing off a cloud of smoke almost the moment they got in. They looked hither and thither and then jumped into the compartment from the upper platform. Some of the compartments were brightly lit up, while the others had a dim shine. Going up, Gora raised his hands and said, 'Come to this side, we will get into the one here.'

Hardly had he spoken than the engine gave out a whistle, and the train started to move even before he could steady his feet. Seizing the handle, with one foot on the footboard, Gora jumped in. 'What's this?' The train had started to move before Gora hardly got in. 'Biju, come hold on to my hand, quick....' he shouted. Biju was small-built, but he jumped onto the train, holding on to Gora's hand. Satu didn't lose a minute and followed suit, hanging onto the handle of the compartment, placing a foot on the footboard. Gora now turned the compartment door handle and, forcing it open, entered the place: it was a first-class compartment with four berths. A middle-aged gentleman wearing dhoti and panjabi now stood up, abandoning his seat. His bespectacled eyes were full of anxiety. Biju followed Gora in. Satu came after them and then he locked the door from the inside. By then, the train was speeding. Satu opened the window for a quick glance outside. There was a look of surprise on his entire face, 'Isn't this the Naihati Local?'

'This is the Lalgola passenger train. It has got in rather late.' The middle-aged person sounded both anxious and irritated.

'What kind of bravado is this that you jump into the compartment from the wrong side of the platform? The locals would have come to a stop, and you do this even without making sure which train it is? How deplorable! Suppose another train had come swishing in upline?'

All the three, Gora, Satu, and Biju, were by now feeling rather ashamed and hassled. Another couple of passengers had got in and were seated, rather well-dressed gentlemen. One with khaki pants and a white half-sleeved shirt tucked in at the waist with knee-length khaki socks and shoes with black laces. He was slightly balding on his pate, the rest of the hair was thin and black—a fat fair man, aged about forty-five years, sitting and frowning at them. The other passenger was thirty or thereabout. He was wearing a dhoti and panjabi, hair wavy and disarrayed, carrying an English daily. He just gave one look at the three and then turned his attention to the newspaper. Biju couldn't help smiling shyly. He rubbed both his hands together and remarked, 'We, of course, did give a thorough look at the upcoming train, but were expecting the one from Naihati, so we thought….'

'The Naihati train is right after ours, the khaki half-pant-clad person's heavy voice sounded a bit gruff now. 'Had it been a local, the train would've come to a stop. But it didn't, did it? It had slowed down because it didn't receive any signal; it hadn't come to a stop. Now better sit down, all of you, rather than fall flat on your faces.'

The three had been standing all this while, the train moving at a terrific speed, swaying, almost dancing as it were; it was not possible to stand straight without holding on to something. They were holding on to each others' hands to prevent themselves from toppling all over the place. They hadn't bought tickets; had decided beforehand they wouldn't. The country was to become independent at daybreak. What was the good in buying tickets? They sat down on the cushioned seats of the first-class compartment. The bespectacled, middle-aged gentleman was seated directly opposite, facing them. The gentleman, wearing half-pant, half-sleeved shirt, wide jaw-boned, and hard-looking, was next to the window. He wore a belt around his waist. On the other hand, the person reading the English daily was seated next to another window on the other side of the compartment, occupying as it were Satu's place. Satu felt that the gentleman wearing shirt could easily go for Charles Laughton, the Hollywood actor, had he been a bit older.

Peering from underneath the spectacles, full of curiosity, the other gentleman asked, 'What is the reason for jumping into a running train like this, taking so much risk?' His tone was mild and inoffensive. Rather, one felt a mix of paternal affection and curiosity in his voice. 'Have you come this side looking for a job? Are you all from Calcutta? Working overtime, that's why the rush, is it not?'

The shirted stocky gentleman now shook with amusement. He did not utter a sound; merely trembled. 'So you think these boys are jute-mill workers? Rushing after doing overtime duty? Can't you see the boys are out on a spree? They had perhaps gone out somewhere and now want to get back to Calcutta in a hurry.'

'No, Sir,' said Biju, assuming one of his inimitable poses. 'We are not returning to Calcutta … and we have not come out to roam here and there either. And besides, except for one, none of us are factory employees. We have certainly not come away doing overtime duty. But we have made a mistake truly, unknowingly taken a risk. However, we are lucky to have got into this Lalgola train. We'll be able to reach Calcutta early.'

The middle-aged gentleman looked despairingly at the half-pant clad and said, 'Can you make any sense of what they say?'

The other shook his head in the negative. 'No, but the boys are not hooligans. This much I can vouch for.'

'That I can see. You are not returning to Calcutta, just going there. Meaning this is where you live. No?' The gentleman interposed.

Satu nodded in assent. 'Yes,' he said. 'We are going to Calcutta, I mean Beliaghata, to Hyderi Mansion.'

There was a look of shock and bewilderment on the bespectacled gentleman's face. 'Why there at this time?' he asked. 'To seek an explanation, again? But that routine was over and done with yesterday.'

'What kind of explanation?' There was a look of utter surprise on Biju's face, as well as in the tone of his voice.

'Yesterday when Gandhiji arrived in Beliaghata from Sodepur, a group of young men, like these (the middle-aged gentleman pointed his fingers at the three of them), raised a slogan saying, "Go back, Gandhiji". They had also entered his room and sought a justification for all he was doing. It was Suhrawardy who had brought Gandhiji to Sodepur all the way from Beliaghata. He would have been probably murdered had he been present.'

'How surprising! I haven't read anything of the sort in the papers,' Gora sounded truly astonished.

'It was reported in *The Statesman*,' the thirty-year-old, occupying the window seat next to them, interjected. 'Some boys assuming a very unpleasant attitude had cornered Gandhiji and asked him why he had dared to come here. "You are full of pity at this little inconvenience caused to the Muslims and have come running here overcome with compassion for them. But where were you when we, the Hindus, were getting killed…." they said. But it must be told that the boys did not stand in the way of Gandhiji entering the Hyderi Mansion, though they did stop Suhrawardy from getting in there. The gentleman there is right. Gandhiji was full of fear that the boys would kill Suhrawardy. He quickly sent Nirmal Bose and others like him to the mansion prior to Suhrawardy's arrival. When Nirmalbabu was entering the place with Suhrawardy, the situation was comparatively quiet. But some young men had managed to somehow enter Gandhiji's room in a state of rage and had told him, "You have come running here to save the Muslims just after four days of minor incidents, but no one was there to save the Hindus from being massacred on August 16 last year,"' thus the young man ended.

'Yes, that was how it happened. He is absolutely right,' the half-pant-clad gentleman now uttered.

'Stop all that, will you!' the middle-aged gentleman shouted at him. 'Must you accept all what those hot-headed youngsters have to tell you? Gandhiji had clearly stated that the situation obtaining that day was vastly different from the one that existed on August 16 the year before. He had said, "I concede that the Muslims were responsible for what took place then. But is now the time to take revenge? I had started the journey with the idea of travelling from Patna to Noakhali. Now I think that if we can maintain peace in this neighbourhood, then I may be able to reach Noakhali. I have not come here only for the Muslims, but for all of you. Everybody is my friend. Today you can choose to kill me or keep me alive. How long can I last, tell me? I had told you as soon as I arrived that if riots start to take place in Noakhali, you must kill me before you raise your hands on the Muslims." But the boys were very angry. They told Gandhiji, "We don't want you to teach us what is violence and what is non-violence." The youth had actually got very angry and told him (Gandhiji), "You better leave this place. We will not allow a single Muslim to enter these regions...."'

By this time, Satu had started biting his nails. Biju was sitting stiffly and Gora listening to all that was being said with a great deal of astonishment. The half-pant-clad gentleman's voice rang out joyfully, 'The boys were right. Did *The Statesman* carry all the news this morning?'

'No, the paper does not mention anything of the sort. And please don't say a word about things you don't understand,' the middle-aged gentleman now got rather agitated. 'I was there yesterday when the events took place,' he continued. 'Gandhiji, seeing how unruly the boys were, said to them, "So you don't want me to intervene, but if you came to my help, you'd see I can create the world anew. You must go to the Muslim area, feeling safe. Don't take them to be your enemies, keeping in mind the events of August 16." A sixteen-year-old boy then got up and intervened, "But history does not record that the Hindus and Muslims, the two communities, have ever lived in peace and friendship side by side. I have seen them fighting ever since I was a child." Just imagine how bad the things had turned that a sixteen-year-old boy, a youngster so to speak, had to say all this. But Gandhi didn't lose patience. He answered, "You aren't older than me, so you haven't heard Hindus address a Muslim as chacha (uncle). You haven't witnessed the two communities coming together socially in the festivals. But leave all that. Do you want that I leave the place? Go away? But I am not prepared to bow down before such dictate. You can imprison me, kill me. I will not call in the troops, or seek the help of anyone. You say that I am the enemy of the Hindus? But that does not distort the truth that resides in my inner soul. How can I accept what you say? If you can convince me of this, I shall leave the place at once of my own accord."'

'And then?' Satu ejaculated, quite unmindful that he had bitten his nails to the point where they were dripping with blood.

'All this continued till almost midnight.' The middle-aged man's voice had now become suffused with emotion. 'Gandhiji said, "Why don't you understand that being a Hindu, I cannot go against my own community, can I? You are all suffering from narrow-mindedness...." These words of Gandhiji worked like magic. All of a sudden, the boys were filled with joy and they took over the entire responsibility of looking after Gandhiji. They began to utter among themselves that the old man was like a magician. Everyone was full of praises for him. He could conquer all minds. Last night, it had turned nine before the prayer or *prarthana* could start....'

The half-pant-clad gentleman now grunted, 'Clever by half, creating a two-day miracle!'

'Take care! You will be thrown out of the compartment of this running train.' Satu's eyes were riveted to the half-pant, half-sleeved shirted man. They were burning!

The looks of the wearer of the half-pant and half-sleeved shirt also evinced signs of anxiety. He turned his eyes towards the middle-aged gentleman, and also the thirty-year-old young man. The train was by then going round a bend, entering the Sealdah station. None of the three blokes had noticed that it had halted in Barrackpore for a considerable time. All of a sudden, Biju blurted out, 'O! There is one question. Why is Lalgola passenger running so late?'

'There was some trouble in Beharampore. Murshidabad is in a state of unrest, so the train was late in starting.' From underneath the glasses, the middle-aged gentleman's eyes appeared to be full of anxiety. 'But one has to go to Beliaghata now,' he said, regarding his watch while removing his shirt sleeve. 'There is no point in waiting for the bus, it's past 8:20. It would be difficult to see him if the prayer meeting is over. Besides, one has to get back.' The train had by then entered the station. Satu smiled, 'Yes, do address us informally. May we know your name?'

The noise of the engine puffing and snarling reverberated in the entire station. The gentleman gave a laugh, 'There is nothing important about my name. I was a Congress worker once. I gave up the party membership a week ago. There is one person I cannot give up. I too will go to Beliaghata with you. But I am not in a hurry; will be spending the night here.'

The three pushed open the door of the compartment. The train had barely stopped when the thirty-year-old young man also moved near the door, and the three jumped out of almost a running train. The young man followed suit and said, 'That gentleman is Aswini Haldar, the leader of the Nadia Congress Party. He has openly spoken against the partition of the country. He says that Nehru and Patel, the two souls, are smitten with Mounbatten. Run now!'

The station hardly had a crowd. Nobody was rushing around the place either. The lights looked somewhat dim. The three came out of the station taking the exit gate. Nobody asked them to show tickets; they couldn't see anyone they knew either. They started running along the road near the Sealdah court, taking a left turn, and ran for sometime without caring for how long. There was a police post outside the Hyderi Mansion—crowds and bright lights. The headlight of an approaching car fell on their faces as they tried to run into the building. Some people pulled them aside, taking hold of their hands, and said, 'Move over. Suhrawardy is coming, bringing Gandhiji along in his car.'

'Suhrawardy driving? Where is he heading?' Satu's voice was trembling. Someone spoke out, 'Gandhiji is going somewhere near the Calcutta lakes; he needs a rest after the day's hard work. He will again be up at three in the morning, as is his wont. Tomorrow is his day of fast.'

The car moved forward; there were lights inside. One could see Suhrawardy at the steering wheel driving past, and someone sitting next to him. Gandhiji, along with Manuben and Abha, were seated at the back of the car. Gandhiji had spectacles on, his dhoti was wrapped around his body like an *odhna* (veil), and his front body bare. Everyone was hailing him. He had both his palms folded next to his bosom in acknowledgement, but his face bore a tired smile.

Satu also raised his palms close to the bosom. He was of the firm belief that he was not an idealist and had no belief in God. There was no question of his adherence to any notion of caste system; he had long back torn and thrown away the sacred thread which hung around his neck. He believed in class struggle. Yet, why was it that his eyes had become moist on seeing the man? Had he forgotton who he was? Had he become unconscious of his identity? Lost a sense of himself?

The car left. Many followed suit, but the crowd was still considerable. Some one from among them said, 'The bastard, he had to admit that he was himself responsible for last year's riots!'

'What do you mean by calling him a bastard?' someone protested in a soft voice. 'If you repeat, I will tear your tongue out. How else could Suhrawardy have acknowledged his culpability? And you are calling him names?'

All grief and grouching that Satu had harboured all these years evaporated the minute he saw Suhrawardy in the role of Gandhiji's charioteer. And next to him and among the crowd, a word was then doing the rounds that a joint procession of five thousand Hindus and an equal number of Muslims led by Aruna Asaf Ali and Ram Monohar Lohia were en route.

Someone from the crowd cried out, 'I will take myself to the Governor's house as soon the procession arrives. At midnight tonight, we will be handed over our right to rule, independent of the British. The event will take place in the Parliament at Delhi.'

Another voice was heard, 'Won't sleep tonight or tomorrow night.'

Satu moved towards the windowless minarets of the Hyderi Mansion. Biju and Gora came after him. Was there the smell of bleaching powder in the air? Some people came and stood barring their way now. One of them spoke out, 'Why are you going in that direction? Can't you see the Mahatma has already left the place?'

'We want to have a look at the room once!' Satu entreated, full of emotions.

The gentleman folded his palms and said, 'Come tomorrow, Sirs. What is there to see? We had kept a simple cot for him; the women were to sleep on the floor. But do you think he would agree to the arrangement? He too slept on the floor. Come tomorrow, you'll see everything—the spinning wheel, the low wooden stool, everything….'

Satu gave a wistful glance at the room, so did Gora and Biju, and then the three of them walked back to the station. All of them were in a hurry to get back. Satu had told Pratima, but the others had not informed their families. Their gait was slow; they were not hurrying like they had been while coming.

'Calcutta is already overcome with the joy of becoming independent, I can see,' Biju took out a cigarette. 'So are we. Now let's have a cigarette!'

There was a note of happy surprise in Satu's voice, 'My heart is full. Do you think Suhrawardy realized his wrongdoing? I am not skeptical of him any more.' He took out the pack of cigarettes from his pocket.

'I am, of course, reminded of that love song.' Gora reached out his hand and took Biju's pack of cigarette while uttering the lines, '*The spring time has cleverly fled lighting up this our earth* … ' There were riots on August 16 last year so that Pakistan became inevitable. Whoever masterminded the event are now successful; they are the ones most happy today.'

Satu gave Gora a fierce nudge in his arm, 'You have uttered what is the actuality, Comrade! Come, smoke one of mine. Return Biju's pack of ciggies.'

All the three reached the Sealdah station, taking quick strides and pulling at their cigarettes. They had got down at the main station while coming, and now they arrived on the north side. A train was about to start. All the three ran towards platform number one.

'Which train is this, Brother?' Gora asked of a passenger seated by the window of the departing train.

'Ranaghat Local,' pat came the reply.

The three got into a first-class compartment after going forward and looking in. They were on a high, experiencing the spirit of independence. But inside the compartment, a small crowd had assembled around someone seated there.

A rather muffled voice uttered, 'Who all have got in? Let me see. Move away a bit, will you?'

'Why have I given up the entire compartment to you both? Go and see why the train is not moving.'

Some moved away. A forty or forty-five-year-old man was sitting, wearing a dhoti and panjabi. He was rather respectable-looking, at least going by the neat and tidy clothes he was clad in. His fine, black-bordered pleated dhoti lay tumbling on the floor. He had on an extra fine handloom panjabi with slim folds and gold buttons, was fair-looking, and had sharp nose, eyes, and a clean-shaven face, but all of these were in a slight disarray. The hair tousled, the parting also gone awry, with bloodshot eyes, he was seated at the window carrying a jute bag, a rather new one. He also held a small and flat bottle in one of his hands with a pint of whiskey in it. There were two others with him, who were not so well-dressed, and looked as if they were his disciples; one of them also with a bottle in his hand. The train left the station, and people jumped out of the moving train, laughing, one among the crowd shouting, 'The drunken bastard!'

'How clever! Calling me a drunken fool!' The elegantly clothed man seated next to the window now remarked, laughing and holding high the whiskey bottle. 'I've been drinking. Won't I get drunk? What new wisdom have you come up with, my dear man!'

The man next to him joined the chorus. 'How right you are, Dada!'

'Will you keep quiet?' the elegantly clad one raised his fingers. You have given you your share, now stay quiet.' He then turned around, looked at Biju, Satu, and Gora, and said, 'Why do you keep standing, Brothers? Sit down, there is so much empty space! Bah, the three of you are so young. To see you is happiness itself, but no! That is not to be. So many ugly faces milling all about us that one's mood is simply destroyed.'

Satu, Biju, and Gora took their seats in the opposite direction. Another person was already seated there. They looked at each other and grinned, all three of them. The situation was nothing new. They had seen many drunkards like him in the past, but the gentleman looked familiar. A person of means, about this there was no doubt. Else, would he have given the same foreign liquor, which he himself was consuming, to others? All of a sudden, a wave of recognition, like a streak of lightning, played inside Satu's brain. He whispered in Biju's ears, 'Arre, he is the same Bidhu Ganguli of Naihati, the famous stage actor.'

By that time, Bidhu Ganguli's hand was already inside the jute bag. One could hear the sound of bottles clashing, and an unopened half pint bottle of whiskey emerged from within. He extended it towards them, calling out to Satu, 'Come, Brothers, take a sip!'

'We don't drink,' Satu tried to sound polite as well as grave.

'Don't we know that?' Bidhu Ganguli gave one of his most endearing smiles. 'One can see by the looks of you that you don't touch these things. But I am giving you some today. You won't sin if you drink today. Before the night is over, we will become free. And it's not that freedom has come to us after a day or two, but after 200 years of a lack of it. There is an ordinance to keep all the liquor shops shut, just imagine! And the foreign liquor shops are closed even on August 16. What kind of an independent country are we living in? Theatre, cinema, radio all will remain open, but the liquor shops? Every one of them will remain shut. What an unholy decision this, tell me, Brothers! Have had to stack up a dozen bottles, the shops remaining closed for the next forty-eight hours. Never mind, I won't suffer if I spare you a bottle. Come on, have a drink!' Bidhu Ganguli almost fell on his feet.

'Believe us,' Biju entreated, his palms brought together. 'We cannot touch the thing with our lips. Or we will fall ill and vomit.'

'How can I explain the sublime attribute of this thing to you, boys?' Bidhu Ganguli now sat up straight. His left hand was holding onto an open bottle. He poured the whiskey neat down his gullet. 'You are both useless,' he said, turning to his two companions. 'Didn't I ask you to fetch a few bottles of soda from the station? But you didn't, did you? All because of money. But would you have to spend from your pockets? You had to just mention my name and the vendor would have let you have them.'

The three companions sat without uttering a word, possibly out of respect, though they had already become slightly inebriated. And now, with the neat whiskey in their stomachs, they had all but lost their voices. Rebuked by Bidhu Ganguli, they continued to sit like morons.

'Know that it would have really made me happy, Brothers,' Bidhu Ganguli said, putting the unopened bottle back into the jutebag. 'One can't do everything with everyone. But if you had given me company then....Freedom not after a day or two, but after 200 years of colonial rule! And our new rulers, our countrymen, they had to go and give orders to close the liquor shops! How can you then drink?'

The person sitting next to him shook his head and said, 'They don't drink these things.'

'Have the boys come and whispered this into your ears?' Bidhu Ganguli scolded him loudly. 'Have I mentioned Gandhiji? I had Prafulla Ghosh in mind. Some people are teetotallers, some aren't. But forbidden to drink on the day of independence is really a shame, quite deplorable! After this, perhaps there will be prohibition in the entire country. What will happen then? People will drink on the quiet, steal it. What do you say, Brothers? Am I saying the untruth?'

The three friends laughed, but didn't add a word. Bidhu Ganguli put the bottle to his lips again and took a long gulp. His face got somewhat contorted, and reddish patches began to appear. He continued to look at the three boys and went on repeating, 'It would have made me very happy had you....'

'We respect you, Sir,' Gora said stretching, puckering his pair of sword-sharp moustache.

'I am reminded terribly of Haru Jetha (Haru Uncle), and if he hadn't turned eighty years old ... ' Biju blurted out.

'I object. This is intolerable,' a low-voiced outburst from Gora.

Bidhu Ganguli raised his folded hands. 'No Brother, don't respect me. Have respect for Sisirdada or Sachindada, the big theatre personalities. I want a little affection. I will be happy for a little love. My wife is very beautiful; she takes good care of me and loves me. Yet I hanker after love,' he raised the bottle all over again and took a sip.

Bidhu Ganguli's words had put to rest whatever internal turmoil Gora and Biju were undergoing. Biju's taste for banter just disappeared, and Gora also forgave him for his poor joke.

The three stared at Bidhu Ganguli's red botched face.

'I haven't uttered the untruth, Brothers,' Bidhu Ganguli continued, nodding his head. 'There is nothing greater than love, Durgada—I mean Durgadas Bannerji with whom I had gone to Dacca to act in plays in 1945. I mean what a lot of adulation and love we received. But what came of all that? If there were love, would the country have got divided? I will not be able to go to Dacca anymore. I don't understand all that—what you call politics, there is no place for love in that and no respect either. Give me a little love.'

August 15, 1947.

'What people say or do are not my concern. I begin my day today by going on a fast. I say it were better we fasted on the day of the birth of a new child or the day of marriage. Fasting is also an inalienable part of feasting, of *bratas* or our rituals. Today we are not only happy; our happiness is mixed with a deep-felt sorrow. Fasting helps us to keep our bodies healthy and our minds pure. And this prayer for purity is also because God may make us worthy of our newly gained freedom.

Today, those of you who are going to rule the country are wearing the crown of rulers. But the throne of power is soiled. That's why you have to be on constant alert, have to be trustworthy, non-violent, and have to have much foresight. The British rule was, in a sense, a trial, but that trial has not ended. You cannot fall prey to fame and wealth. May God bless you. You must look after the poor and the rural folks.

Today is the first day of independence. The ordinary masses thought that the palace of the Governor General now belonged to them, that was why they had ruthlessly taken possession of it. It is true that all people have the right to enter that palace. But it is also matter of regret that because the British have left, we think we can commit the place to rack and ruins. One cannot condone such a barbarous act. If we can bring back the power and strength of unity we witnessed during the Khilafat Movement, we will taste nectar or rather the poison we are about to consume. People crowded all about the place when Gandhiji came out on the streets of Calcutta at 8 o'clock that night. He was greeted by Jai Hind in the largely Muslim area. How the little boys and girls hung about the place dying to touch his hands!

Satu, Biju, and Gora returned to the station at quarter to ten at night after witnessing such scenes.

They had decided, when going to Satu's for their midday meal, that they would be going to East Pakistan on the day itself. At first, Pratima had thought the three had gone mad. They had lain on a mattress, lighting a cigarette. In the single room in Satu's house after they had eaten, Gora almost jumped up and sat, saying, 'But, I had told her that I would sit with her and listen to the radio. Such good programmes today: Pankaj Mullick, Jaganmoy Mitra, Hemanta Mukhopadhyay, Suchitra Mukhopadhyay, Supriti Ghosh, and Bijon Ghosh Dastidar, songs of Atul Prasad, Najrul and Rabindra Sangeet, Shishir Bhadhuri's recitations of poetry, and the reading of Sachin Sengupta's play *Swadhin Bharat* (India Independent)! I cannot come with you, dear brothers.'

Satu let go a puff of smoke. 'So don't come. We'll leave in sometime. Will visit Beliaghata first and decide which train to get into after listening to Gandhiji's talk. We will get into any mail or express train we come across.'

'Then let me go and take a look around my home first,' Biju too had sat up. 'If nothing else, at the least let Ma know about it.'

'Yes, you simply must,' Satu had concurred.

'In which case, I will have to let Baba know too,' Gora's voice was trembling like the sound of cuddled milk.

Satu, laughing and glancing meaningfully at Biju, said, 'And must you not let Sudhaboudi know?'

'Of course, I have to,' Gora's voice sounded rather sharp. 'I have already indicated that. Will it be nice if I come away without telling her?'

Biju blew out a smoke ring. 'Not at all. We would have had to tell her had you not.'

'You son of a bitch!' Gora laughed.

It was only a single room attached to a verandah with a tiny kitchen in which they sat eating, while Pratima listened to all that they were saying. A ten- or twelve-year-old girl was Pratima's help in running the household. In reality, her main job was looking after the child. There she stood, a rather dark-looking girl with the baby in her arms, the child gurgling and making all kinds of noises, bending down to touch Pratima. Biju and Gora had come out of the place ere they finished taking their meal. It had been decided that they would appear at the station at 4 pm sharp.

By the time Pratima re-entered the room, after washing her hands beside a well, Satu was lying on his side, his eyes half shut.

'Sleeping?' Pratima asked.

'No,' he said with a sleepy voice. 'Where's the child?'

Pratima was looking outside the building. 'Kali has gone roaming in the neighbourhood, taking the child along with her.'

'Have you eaten?'

'Yes.'

'Why not shut the door?'

'What for?'

'All that rot!'

'Don't pull my leg; I'm not in the mood.'

Satu was bare-bodied; a freshly laundered dhoti was tied like a lungi around his waist. He turned to his side and was gazing at Pratima, laughing, 'How can you be in a good mood? Why not close the door?'

Pratima's hair was loose, untied; she had just had her bath, and was wearing an ordinary saree with grey stripes on, and a blouse of the colour blue. Her eyes betrayed signs of complaint and offense. She looked steadily at Satu standing against the door. It was Satu who had pulled her in laughing and had locked the door. Their room was on the ground floor of a large house; the courtyard was to their front and across were two other tenants. The two windows of the room were already shut. Once the door was closed, the room turned almost pitch dark. Satu pulled Pratima to his bosom, and Pratima, though trying hard to extricate herself from his embrace, became more entangled in his.

'I am not enjoying this. Leave me alone,' she said.

'Why are you not liking all this? That's exactly what I would like to know.' Satu made her sit up on the mattress, putting his arms around her, and gave her a kiss. 'Unhappy because I am going to Pakistan, are you? Good, I won't go if you do not wish that.'

Though the room was dark, because the doors and windows were shut, there was some light streaming in from the two netted openings on the wall, creating a play of light and shade. Pratima was looking intently at Satu, her eyes betraying anxiety. 'Who knows what's going on in Pakistan? You want to go? Suppose there is trouble.'

'Nothing untoward is likely to happen at this juncture,' Satu's voice was full of a calm reassurance. 'Now all are enjoying to the hilt at the newly earned freedom. Haven't you seen in the papers that the Hindus and Muslims are holding peace meetings at different places in East Pakistan?' Saying this, Satu drew Pratima even closer to his bosom, but failed to allay her fears. The papers had other kind of news as well. That the Hindus had run away from many places abandoning their hearth and homes. They had sent their wives and daughters away to the so-called 'safe places'. That meant there was enough trouble. 'I am very scared,' Pratima rejoined.

'We will be back forthwith if we see anything like that happening,' Satu tried to explain. 'We are, after all, three free grown-up men, but we do want to once see what kind of place the country has become as Pakistan. Don't be anxious or afraid.' Satu took Pratima's face close to his and planted a kiss on her lips. It made Pratima feel less worried. But she had a grouse. She said, 'Once out of the house, you forget everything about it. You don't have any feelings. To live with someone like you is to forever remain in a state of anxiety.'

'What strange talk is this? How can I go away leaving you behind?' Satu laughed his heart out. 'You think I have no feelings for you? How could you say such things—oh, oh, you are perspiring so, dear Kusi!'

Pratima's pet name was Kusi. She put her hand on Satu's bosom and uttered, 'You are also perspiring. Let me bring the hand-fan and fan you. Try to get some sleep.'

Satu and Pratima went to sleep in each other's arms. Both were perspiring heavily, taking deep breaths; their touching each other, holding together in close embrace, taking deep kisses took their longing to that inevitable conclusion where their mutual need was fulfilled. Pratima got up after fifteen minutes and opened the door. Satu went on sleeping, turning to his side. Pratima found Kali sitting under the shade of the verandah, the child asleep on her lap. She took the sleeping child off her lap and put it next to the somnolent Satu. She then fanned them both with her hand-fan and watched them sleeping.

Satu was a light sleeper. He was up in about an hour's time. By that time, a tired Pratima had fallen into a deep slumber, the hand-fan still in her grasp. Satu looked up at the timepiece placed on the shelf. It was 3:40. Satu was quietly putting on his pant and shirt, preparing to run a comb through his hair in front of the mirror resting on the niche of the wall, when Pratima woke up. She was embarassed. Despite the fact she had had so much to do since the wee hours of the morning.

Satu took out some rupee notes and gave it to Pratima saying, 'There's thirty rupees.'

'But you haven't kept any money for yourself, have you?'

'I have. Just a matter of few days. We will be leaving in one train, and returning by another in a day's time. We are not going to be roaming around the town, looking up places. Just a glimpse of a new country to see how new it looks.'

'But I am apprehensive. I am afraid.'

Satu held Pratima up with his two hands, 'Nothing to be afraid of, Kusi. It's getting late, let me go,' he said, touching her cheeks with his lips. He was about to give a kiss to his sleeping child as well when Pratima brushed him aside saying, 'What are you doing? Musn't kiss a child who is asleep.'

That was something! A superstition and a belief in the occult. It was not right to kiss a sleeping child or the elders when they are not awake. It was like paying respect to a corpse; it was a sign of death. Satu rushed out of the room, shouting back, 'I have to go.'

He reached the station exactly at 4 o'clock. Biju was waiting. The Kanchrapara Local was due at 4.15.

Gora was yet to arrive. He came running a minute before the train got in, panting away.

The precincts of the Sealdah main station were dressed up in lights. The Governor's palace, Writers' Building, and other big new offices in Netaji Road were also illuminated. Only yesterday, Charnock Place, Clive Street, and Dalhousie Square had been named after Netaji. Satu arrived at the station and lit a cigarette. 'Can't make head or tail of what this new independent government is upto. Earlier it had announced that the partition of the country would make so many people unhappy that it would be improper to decorate the place with lights. Now I find it is exactly the reverse.'

'Except for one person, everybody else has forgotten that there is a sense of deep sorrow amidst all the joy.' Biju, taking a matchstick out of Satu's box of matches, continued, 'Seeing Calcutta like this, do you feel that the country has been torn apart?'

Gora didn't light his cigarette, though he had taken one out, and said, 'Come, we may find the same situation where we are about to go. In that, everybody is in the seventh heaven at the joy of becoming free.'

All the three entered the main station through its wide open gate of entry. They saw a couple of black-coated ticket collectors moving about here and there. Nobody seemed to bother. Music was floating in from the nearby microphone, possibly installed inside the Sealdah market. The GRP sentries were gathered together in a corner, laughing and confabulating among themselves. The city of Calcutta seemed to be caught up in joy, the station empty of crowds. The three walked in the eastern direction where all the lamps had not been lit up. A train was stationary there, the compartments, though full of passengers, mostly dark. One could not see the faces of the travellers in the dim light, though some hung out of carriage windows, gazing in their direction. One had the feeling that that their eyes and faces belied fear. The other travellers looked distinctly suspicious of the three of them.

A couple of gun-trotting policemen came near and stood in front of the three now. They asked in Hindi, 'What are you doing here?'

'Nothing much,' Gora replied with a sprinkling of Hindi. 'We are looking for our train.'

The armed policeman said, 'There's no train for you in this platform. This train is full of Muslim passengers. They are being packed off to East Pakistan. It's a special coach, please go elsewhere.'

The three looked at each other. And looked again at the train. That meant all the passengers in the train were homeless Muslims from Calcutta in distress. Perhaps, all were destitutes of a wrecked slum. Could this be the special train carrying the wretched refugees of the Canal West Road? The air in Calcutta was resounding with the slogan of 'Hindu–Muslim Bhai Bhai', although this could not be heard from where they were. But what would be the attitude of the passengers once they reach East Pakistan? Satu had already raised the question the day before. Won't their jaws stiffen?

The three went further west. There was a rather long train stationary there. Two uniformed ticket collectors were also standing there. Satu went near them and asked, 'Tell me, Dada, which train is this one?' 'North Bengal Express,' the fat, rather fair ticket collector replied. 'Where would you be going?' Biju laughed. 'We are going to take a look at East Pakistan,' he said.

'East Pakistan?' The other ticket collector, rather thin and dark, looked up at them in surprise and asked, 'Are you Hindus?'

'Yes,' Gora nodded.

'Then why this sudden fancy to travel to East Pakistan?' the fat ticket collector asked.

Satu smiled, 'We've seen Hindustan, so thought we'd go and see what the new country is like.'

'Then, I guess this is the train you have to take; it'll be leaving right now. It is already late by five minutes; was supposed to start at 10 pm, but....'

The fat ticket collector waved his index finger and addressed Satu informally as 'you'. 'Okay, dears, go; but be careful. The district magistrate of Nadia has been imposing wholesale penalty on the Hindus. Murshidabad ought to have been left in India. Now the rumour goes that Pakistan flags are flying in Murshidabad.'

'Not only that,' the other collector, the thin dark one added, sounding really frightened. 'The goods train running through Kusthia, Natore, Gopalpur, Shantahar line are being looted daily, and the villages nearby robbed. Don't you know about all this?'

Biju let out a ring of smoke, 'We've read something like this in the papers, but there was also much good news. Since we are on our way....'

The bell rang loudly ere he could finish his sentence.

'Is that the warning bell?' Gora looked back, suddenly alarmed.

'There is nothing like a warning bell or something similar here; this is final,' the fat ticket collector said, pointing to the train. 'It will leave right now. Go in quickly and take your seats. The train is going empty; you will be able to sleep comfortably. Go, go and see the new country. You couldn't have bought tickets, isn't that so?'

Satu nodded, giving a smile.

The ticket collectors laughed in unison, though not in the same tone. The thin one had a deep voice, the fat one like a child's. The fat and fair one shook in laughter. 'Clever, aren't you?'

'Now climb into the compartment, and come back in one piece. May Goddess Durga protect you!' The thin one raised his two hands and touched the forehead.

The train's whistle blew. Satu and Biju strode forward, following the train. Biju had on a folded jute shawl on his shoulders and was carrying a small bag of coarse white linen. Gora however couldn't keep pace with his friends; he was looking back at the two ticket collectors again and again, on the night of August 14. How different Sealdah station looked from Calcutta! A train like the North Bengal Express—one of the fastest trains—was leaving the station without any passengers. The station had no people milling in the place; some compartments were not even lit up. Surprise, surprise! The light in some compartments was so dim that one couldn't see the passengers through the open windows. There were some people in the third- and inter-class compartments; however, the first and second class, though lit up, had none.

'I swear by Mary, the Mother of God, I don't like this one bit,' Gora's discomfiture now found expression in the tone of his voice. 'This train will run through the Nadia district. According to the new ordinance promulgated in Murshidabad, all meetings and processions are banned in Kandi sub-division till August 28. Lord knows what kind of trouble is brewing there. We know absolutely nothing about all this....'

Gora had hardly finished his sentence, when the whistle began to blow even more shrilly. The wheels of the train went round making a crashing sound and started to move. Satu jumped into the first compartment he could find, his hand on the handle and his foot on the pedestal. But the door was shut from the inside. He hadn't noticed that it was a first-class compartment, nor saw how many people were seated inside. A gentleman donned in khaki pants and twill white half-sleeved shirt now jumped up from his seat and opened the door. Satu stumbled in, followed by Biju and Gora.

The gentleman gaped at the three friends, wonderstruck. Strongly built, darkish in colour, the man seemed close to fifty. His face was clean-shaven, his hair thin and balding, but he had a sharp nose and eyes that lit up with intelligence. He held an almost burnt-out Burmese cheroot with a couple of his fingers. There was no doubt that the man had a distinct personality. The three friends were quite oblivious of the fact that they had jumped into the moving train, that the gentleman had himself got up and let them in, and they hadn't given a thought to shutting the door after them. The gentleman had performed that duty, turning the lock in rather firmly. His wife was probably seated in the lower bunk, and had a gown on. Satu, Biju, and Gora called that kind of a dress 'gown'. The lady had bobbed hair, shoulder-length tresses. Her bright brownish looks, however, resembled any other Bengali woman, though in the eyes of the three friends, she was indeed a memsahib. There were two young sixteen- or eighteen-year-old girls sitting at the other end of the compartment. They too were dressed like the woman. One had a pink dress on, and the other a dress of soft strawberry colour. Both brownish-looking with shoulder-length hair. The woman and the girls had painted their lips red. There was, therefore, no doubt at all that they were memsahibs. All had watches on their wrists. The women did not wear jewellery, but had high-heel sandals on their feet.

The two fans rotating above the compartment ceiling wafted in a mild breeze, redolent of a foreign perfume. One heard the gentleman mention *Evening in Paris* frequently, prior to the Great War, but one got to hear many more different names now that the war was over. The three could not distinguish the particular smell hovering in the air. There was no question that the scent belonged to some eau de cologne which formed a part of their toiletries.

The two bunks above were already unfolded, made ready for bed. These had both linen sheets and a couple of cushions placed there as well. One look at these told them that they were kept ready for sleeping. Biju, Satu, and Gora were left standing uncomfortably, uncertain as to what they would do. The gentleman took on a serious air and said with a deep voice in English, looking at the girls, 'You two come and sit on this side.' The girls soon enough joined the woman who was seated opposite. They looked extremely irritated. Both were chewing something, perhaps chewing gum. There were suitcases stuffed below the bunks. A steel trunk too large to be pushed underneath the bunk was placed at one end which had the name MR G. MILLER written in capital letters with a white paint. And below, the name of the place: CALCUTTA, SYEDPORE.

The gentleman, no doubt Mr Miller himself, now betook himself on an empty window seat, looked up at the friends, and said with a mild Yankee accent, 'Why keep standing? Do take a seat.'

They behaved as if they were waiting for the gentleman's order, and sat down as soon he uttered the words. Gora took out his cigarette pack and held it out to his friends. Satu and Biju knew that Gora was showing off, deliberately adopting a pose, in order to impress the gentleman and his wife. Else, Gora was not likely to be so generous for no reason at all. He was carrying besides his shawl, a big paper packet filled with necessary items. He didn't say what these were. Only Satu did not have anything to carry. He was wearing an American soldier's khaki pants, a full-sleeved, maroon-coloured shirt, socks, and blue-coloured canvas shoes. Biju wore a pyjama and panjabi, while Gora a dhoti and shirt.

They had gone to the Nakhoda Masjid to savour the freely distributed pink-coloured liquid. It had already become late by the time they had arrived, and the affair of the sherbet had come to an end. The arrangement was primarily for the Hindus a gesture of friendship to celebrate communal unity, though there were Muslims there too galore. And the slogan, 'Hindu–Muslim Bhai Bhai' had rented the air. They had then eaten kebabs and tandoori bread at a Muslim restaurant.

The three friends now lit up their cigarettes. Gora and Satu did not make a mistake when eyeing the ashtray, but had no wish really to come face to face with either the mother or the girls. Nevertheless, their eyes refused to be tamed. Just then, the gentleman, Mr Miller, brought out his shiny petrol lighter from out of his shirt pocket and lit his cheroot. Biju raised up his mouth and blew out a ring of smoke and laughed, remarking, 'The ticket collectors were something really! No?'

'You are perhaps travelling to Naihati, are you?' The gentleman turned towards them, his tone amiable and extremely polite. He spoke in English.

Satu shook his head in the negative. 'No, Sir,' he uttered humbly, 'we are not sure how far we would go. The country has been partitioned; we are going to the other portion of the country that has been divided.'

'Which means you are travelling to East Pakistan?' The gentleman forgot to give a pull at his cigar. He then took a sharp turn, faced them, and asked, 'You are Hindus, no?'

Gora let the cigarette dangle in his mouth. 'Yes, but why ask? Is there something to worry about?'

'Probably not. In any case, this is something I cannot tell.' The gentleman appeared as if taken by surprise. 'But today, everybody is caught up celebrating his or her becoming a part of an independent nation. You three, I can quite realize, are the young sons of educated Bengali Hindu families. How these thoughts come to your heads is something I cannot understand. Do you possess land and property in East Pakistan? Are you going there for this or are you visiting some relatives?'

Biju shook his head and gave a polite smile as if in respect.

'We may be having some relatives there,' he said. 'We are not in the know about it. We are not visiting anybody in particular; you have just said that the entire country is celebrating its freedom, and you are not in the wrong saying this. We three friends have made up our minds that the way to celebrate our independence would be to find out what the new country is like. We want to see how the people there are celebrating their freedom. That is why the three of us have ventured out....'

'Wonderful, wonderful,' exclaimed the gentleman, pulling at his half-extinguished cheroot in a futile manner. He gave a smile, his pair of tobacco-stained teeth intact, and quickly glanced at the opposite seats. His voice was a mix of laughter and amusement, 'Well well, since you don't have any particular destination, you couldn't have bought any tickets, I guess?'

Satu blew out a puff of smoke. 'How true,' he said. 'We have indeed not bought any tickets. Today we are fully free!'

'Free? What do you mean exactly? Enjoying on becoming an independent nation?' The gentleman roared in laughter. 'You are free, so are we. We too have gained independence. But does that mean we can travel by train without buying tickets? There is good reason to cheat the British and travel free of charge. But the situation is not the same now. From today, this railway is the company of our independent nation.'

Biju bent down and emptied the ashtray. 'You have said the correct thing, Sir,' he rejoined. 'This railway now belongs to our independent nation. But please don't think that we are in the habit of ticketless travelling. We haven't been buying tickets since yesterday, not only today. This is to be our first and last ticketless travel by train. We don't wish to lie to you. There is a taste of freedom in not buying the ticket which we are savouring....'

'The taste of freedom in ticketless travel!' the gentleman repeated amusingly. 'A very dangerous sense of pleasure indeed! The only hope is, as you say, that these are the first and last days of your travelling without tickets. Of course, I have the idea that no one will be coming to you asking you to show your ticket today, or for a few days; everybody like you all are perhaps caught up in celebrating freedom. Besides, there is a saying in Hindi, '*Sarkar ki mal darya ki dhal*' (pour down the drain what belongs to the authorities). This is also a habit of most government servants. But we have to change that particular mindset from today. We are no longer under a foreign rule; we are an independent nation. We are free. No one will come asking for a ticket from you today. Even if they do, who is there to book you? But the passengers of buses and trams are still having to pay their fees. I am sure the movies are not being screened without charge. The eateries not selling eatables free of charge. But I have to admit that there is much novelty in your stance.'

Satu cleared his throat. He smiled weakly, though rather embarrassed. 'But Sir, you must have bought your ticket, no?'

'I have been lecturing you all this while. How could you think after all this that I am travelling in a first-class compartment with my family without buying tickets?' He turned serious. It was clear that he was a bit angry at Satu's question. 'I am an officer of the railways, the foreman of Syedpore Railway Factory, travelling with official railway pass.'

Satu did not lose time to admit his mistake, 'I am very guilty, Sir, sorry. Should not have asked you such a question. I am asking all of you to forgive me.' Then turning around and giving the three individuals seated on the opposite bunk a quick look, he asked, 'I guess, you are Mr G. Miller?'

'Yes, I am G. Miller, an Anglo-Indian. Have been in Syedpore Railway Factory from its inception. Have you heard of Syedpore?' He gave a look at the black steel trunk bearing his name.

Biju and Gora immediately nodded their heads. They said they did, and so did Satu. 'We've heard about it, Sir. Is it placed in Rangpur district?'

'No, no,' Mr Miller shook his head vigorously. 'It falls within the Dinajpur district. The Boundary Commission hasn't as yet made up its mind about the western and eastern parts of the district. But this much is certain that the whole of Dinajpur will not fall within the ambit of any one country. There is no way out but to halve the district into eastern and western parts. I go on hearing all kinds of rubbish rumours. It is difficult to distinguish truth from falsehood among these, though it is without doubt that Syedpore belongs to the eastern half of the district, rubbing its shoulders against the border of Rangpur district. There is a strong likelihood that it will go to East Pakistan. The Muslims have demanded the entire Dinajpur district, but I don't believe that it will come about. The Balurghat and Raiganj regions are Hindu majority areas. Whatever, I have been ordered to get back to Syedpore today itself. But I will return to India for sure. Even now, there are so many Hindus there. I mean in the railway factory. I know that so far no one has been ordered to leave the place and come away. But everyone is prepared mentally for that eventuality. There were no riots there; whatever skirmishes that have taken place are very inconsequential indeed. There is a suppressed anxiety everywhere, I guess. But Syedpore is such a place, because of the presence of the railway workshop, that people from all over the country may be found there—Hindus, Muslims, Christians, all. Besides, for a few days now, we will all be besotted by the idea of freedom. The people in East Pakistan too would be full of joy at becoming a newly independent nation. And that great pilgrim, don't mind, young man, because I think Mahatma Gandhi is the great pilgrim to Calcutta. Calcutta has offered itself to him.' Then, suddenly looking out of the window, he exclaimed, 'Which station is this one? Are we leaving Barrackpore behind?' The woman sitting opposite him shook her head and said, 'Yes.'

'I have reserved this four-berthed, first-class compartment,' the gentleman added, raising his wrist to note the time on his wristwatch. 'I must say that the driver of our train is hardly going slow, ecstatic as he is with joy at becoming independent! The North Bengal Express is speeding to keep its reputation intact. Our dinner is over; we are going to get some sleep. You should get down when the train arrives at Naihati station. You will find other first-class compartments going empty. I have seen to that. Will be able to travel enjoying the spirit of free India.'

Biju bent low and stubbed his cigarette end in the ashtray and said, 'Mr Miller, rest assured we would certainly leave this compartment and get into another one when the train arrives in Naihati. We got into this one in Sealdah, unknowingly. We are sorry to have caused you inconvenience.'

'Thanks.' Mr Miller smiled and glanced at the others opposite to him and said to the lady, 'Such nice boys, they are!'

The lady agreed. Though not introduced, it was not difficult to make out that she was Mrs Miller. The two young girls were their daughters. Gora stubbed his cigarette into the ashtray. There was a distinct sign of discomfiture on his face and eyes. He looked at Mr Miller and asked, 'Mr Miller, when did you arrive in Calcutta?'

'About ten days ago,' Mr Miller was curious. 'Not in Calcutta exactly, I had come to Icchhapore,' he continued. 'My only son works in the Icchhapore Rifle Factory. He has just been posted as the new supervisor of the barrel section. Of course, I had taken leave from work so that I could come and see for myself. Who knows when I can come to India again, or where they would be sending me to? I am afraid I could learn nothing, I had a fortnight's leave, but I am having to rush back after getting a telegram from Syedpore. Would you be knowing why?'

He looked at the faces of the three boys. Satu and Biju were also wondering what Gora had to say. Gora turned to Mr Miller. 'You are an Anglo-Indian. I am sure the Muslims have no headaches about the people of your community,' he said. 'And to tell the truth, we have absolutely no idea what is happening or where we are going. There is no one in that place like Mahatma Gandhi, whom you call a pilgrim, whose presence can drive out all evil powers like magic. You have come away from that country only ten days ago, therefore I ask you for your advice. Should we be going to that country?'

'Look, it is a question I have no answer to,' Miller took out his shiny lighter and lit a cigar. 'There was some trouble at Dinajpur, but that was quickly taken care of. I read in the papers that the trouble had its roots in Radcliffe's uncertainty as to where the region belonged. But, of course, I don't know where you are heading for, though you've got into the North Bengal Express. There are several junctions on the way. You can change your train and go to the east or the south-east, whichever direction you choose. You can even reach Noakhali. But I cannot tell you anything about Noakhali or Dacca. And to tell the truth, I have simply no idea what kind of welcome awaits you or where you may go in East Pakistan. But a lot of Hindus still remain in that country. Some have run away, no doubt; there are some rumours to that effect. I have witnessed no riots in Syedpore, though I have heard that some rich Hindus of Dinajpur are trying to buy off land in the western part of the region.

'This is something I do not understand.' Satu looked up at Mr Miller in surprise, 'That someone can buy off a large piece of land with money. Who will take the money? Who is it meant for? Who are to be bribed?'

'What an extraordinary thing you have said, young man,' a heavy pungent smoke from Mr Miller's cigar filled up the entire compartment. He laughed loudly, 'People talk of money, they mention the unfair decision of Radcliffe. But who all are taking the money, or who are being bribed? I do not have a clue about all these. Have you heard nothing about the cash transactions?'

Gora jerked his shoulders. 'I have. The papers never carry this kind of news. I heard about it from a particular Muslim gentleman lawyer, a leader of the Muslim League Party too, that the Hindu rich zemindars are trying to keep Khulna inside India by raising three crores of rupees. He perhaps knows who the money is meant for, but he didn't mention that.'

'Now we can understand that in the situation, a lot of uncertainties emerge regarding East and West Bengal. In this case, what kind of advice can I give you, tell me?' Mr Miller turned very grave. 'But you are not correct in saying that the Muslims pose no worry before us. I wonder who has? Do you have any worry on that score? It is true we never say a thing about the partition of the country. I know little how much importance or value is given to the opinion of our representative, I mean of the Anglo-Indian community. Nevertheless, I would like to state something directly without demurring, that is I get very frightened when I hear of communal rioting. You see, I have those two young girls I am sure I would have had to fear nothing had I lived in Calcutta. And if you ask me about my mental attitude, I am in favour of staying back in India. If you hear how our young boys and girls (the Anglo-Indians) talk, you'd think they would be happy stepping into the shores of England. How absurd! They talk as if England is their motherland. Nonsense! India is our country. We want to stay here. Some may want to emigrate to Pakistan, and if the constitution of Pakistan recognizes our rights, then it will be good. India already has—' He stopped, then pulling a few times at the near-extinguished cigar and blowing out smoke, he said, 'I don't think you can land into any deep trouble. Like you, all the people here too are rapt in joy at their new independence. That does not mean I can connect these people with the Hindus of East Pakistan. It is true that although there are no tensions in places like Rangpur or Syedpore, the Hindus have no sense of peace in their mind. Peace and a sense of security are returning to the minds of the Muslims of Calcutta; but what of the Muslims in Bihar? Is there any peace left in their minds?' He pulled at the cigar again, blew out smoke, and smiled. 'There is no question that it is a matter of great happiness that the country is becoming independent after so many years, but is there really any happiness?'

Gora's face darkened. The train had reduced its speed after hurtling away. There was not a drop of assurance in what Mr Miller had to tell the boys. He could not give them any hope. How could he? He had frankly admitted his anxieties regarding his two young daughters. And that had he stayed in Calcutta, he wouldn't have had any worries on that score. The three friends were yet to decide whether they would go to Noakhali or Dacca. In fact, they hadn't decided at all where they would be going. They were going to see a country divided anew. That was in itself their way of celebrating the joy of attaining freedom. The North Bengal Express was about to start its journey when they arrived at the Sealdah station. They got into it. But the country they were going to had as its Dacca capital. It was but natural that they would be attracted to it, though they also knew that they would not be able to reach Dacca on this express train.

'I think we are arriving at Naihati,' Mr Miller remarked, his eyes directed outside the compartment. 'The look of the yard tells me that, but one thing surprises me … ' he turned around to take another look at his friends. 'It's good that you are going to see a new country. I can't see any luggage with you. Where are your clothes?'

Satu laughed and shook his head, 'We haven't brought any. Will manage with the clothes we have in the few days we spend here.'

'You are talking like vagabonds,' Mr Miller gave a laugh. 'Although you all look as if you belong to respectable well-to-do families. You could have have brought some extra clothes in a suitcase. How long can you live in these?'

Biju smiled, 'How right you are … but we have been thinking that, if necessary, we will buy some clothes. I am sure we can do that in that country.'

'Of course!' Mr Miller now gave a resounding laughter. He gave the opposite bunk another look and said, 'I can see you have money with you, but it's better not to broadcast the fact. I can assure you this much now—you can safely travel to East Pakistan for some days. The ordinary people are happy. The Muslim supervisor of the staff of the workers had told me ten days before I had left that they were looking forward to happy days. And how was it that I was leaving? One Bihari Muslim used to invite me for Eid, the Muslim festival, each year. He could make extraordinary beef steaks. I am sure he is doing that today. He had told me about it. But my mind was elsewhere, although nothing came out of nothing. The manager's wire arrived, "Join tomorrow." Lord knows what's in store for me!'

The train came to a stop at Naihati station. The three friends got up from their seats and said, 'Goodnight!'

'Goodnight,' Mr Miller stood up and extended his hand. 'It has been a pleasure knowing you,' he said.

Pleasure knowing them? Perhaps it was a sense of relief that one felt after a strong assurance that made a person utter these words. Mr Miller had hardly got to know the three friends; he didn't even know their names, didn't want to either. He also knew that he was a sahib (didn't belong to them). Nevertheless, as an Anglo-Indian, he had opened out his heart to them. Especially about the Anglo-Indian phobia about England. The three friends turned around to give a last look at Mrs Miller and the girls before getting down. They all had a smile on their face. Especially Mrs Miller—a smile of supreme satisfaction. The three dropped into the platform. Mr Miller shut the door after bidding them a second goodnight. He pulled down the window shutters as well.

Platform number three of the Naihati station. The shops were all lit up, but there were hardly any people, no passengers getting in or getting off the train. This despite the fact it was the North Bengal Express. A train that took you to the furthest end of North Bengal. There are several junction stations on the way. From Kusthia station, one could take another train to Jessore or Faridpore. One could as well get into a steamer from Faridpur Rajbari (the zemindar's house) and arrive at Dhaka, the capital of East Pakistan. One could go to Dacca through Pabna and Sirajgunj from Ishwardi, and then taking the steamer to Jagganathgunj to travel by train to Mymensingh. And if one went straight north, one could pass by Natore-Rajshahi, Shantahar, Bagora, Pataliputra, and Jalpaiguri, though Jalpaiguri was no longer a part of East Pakistan. Perhaps, North and East Dinajpur formed the border. After that, it was like going endlessly eastward....

'The train will stop for five minutes, one hopes,' Satu lit up a cigarette. 'I am dying of hunger. Couldn't we stuff ourselves with something?'

'We must,' Biju shook his head. 'But what can we find here? It is almost eleven in the night. But let's go there. There's a fire lit. Maybe they are frying something,' Biju pointed northwards.

Gora was seen talking to a person, perhaps someone he knew. Seeing Satu and Biju advancing in the northward direction, he called out to the gentleman, 'Why not come along? I have two friends with me. You can talk to them.'

Satu asked, looking back while walking, 'What will he tell us?'

The man was tall and dark, and had a dirty dhoti and shirt on. He smiled at Satu, 'What new thing can I say? Haven't you read in the papers that many Hindus have already come away to Naihati from Pakistan? There are a few families staying on platform number one, though they are not poor. They are looking for a suitable land to buy going round like mad, and hunting for rooms to rent until they find one. But what was inevitable in the circumstances was that the house rents have climbed up, hit the ceiling, and along with it the price of land. Can you imagine that they are asking for rupees five hundred for a kottah of land in a place like Naihati? Even the papers have reported this.'

'Gora, did you read about it in the papers?' Satu asked, stopping in front of a tea stall.

Biju's voice can now be heard in a sing-song tone, saying, 'Satu dear, they are frying some puris! But one cannot eat standing here. Let's buy and take some; there are sweets too.'

'Do that,' Satu pulled at his cigarette, blowing out smoke from his nose and lips. Then turning to Gora he said, 'I think I read about it five or six days ago in the papers.'

Gora, however, shook his head; he hadn't. 'In any case,' he said, 'there's time enough to ponder. We can return home from Naihati in a cycle rickshaw. I don't like what I hear.'

'Then it were better you went back,' Satu went near Biju. 'We have got into North Bengal Express; won't get off anywhere in the night. We will decide where we are going when it is dawn and we are awake. There is nothing we can see in the dark of the night. I doubt whether we can see anything at all when the train arrives at Kusthia passing by Kestonagar. The city of Dacca is a different matter. It is a capital city; there would be rejoicing there night-long like Calcutta.

'Listen,' Biju gave Satu's shirt a tug, 'the man selling the puris is saying that we can quickly have our food. It is time for the train to leave. He says we should not drink water from the train's bathrooms. Should I ask him to serve us hot?'

'Why not? Let us eat before we go.' Gora threw down his cigarette and crushed it under his shoes.

The puri-seller gave them hot puris and vegetables in a little bowl made of sal leaves. Gora took the bowl from off his hands, but didn't gobble up the food like Biju and Satu did.

The puri-seller twirled his moustache and smiled and said, 'It won't cost you much. Give me two annas, I'll supply you with a pitcher full of fresh water. Where will you find it if you get thirsty at night?'

Biju looked askance at Gora while he ate and said, 'I won't say a thing. You tell him. I don't want to be blamed if anything goes wrong.'

'Eat eat, you rascal. You think that only you have fear for life? We don't?' Satu scolded. 'It's all the same if we were to fall into the hands of hoodlums no matter where. In which case there wouldn't be any difference between West Bengal and East Pakistan. But didn't you hear what Mr Miller finally had to say? That we are full of joy, but there they don't feel any such thing. Are they lying in wait for us so that they can kill us as soon as we get in there?'

Gora was by then beginning to eat his puris. He whined, 'I haven't even once said that I'll leave you and go away. I felt bad after hearing what had taken place at Naihati. It's no use courting danger while we celebrate. Is there?'

'I don't believe we can ever be in danger,' Satu said, his mouth full of puris and veggies. His voice sounded ugly. He gulped the food and cleared his throat and continued, 'And to tell the truth, we are going there to enjoy, aren't we? To have fun. We should all feel like pilgrims.'

The dirty dhoti and shirted man had been standing next to them all this while. He gave a rather strange quick laugh, as if like the neighing of a horse. 'Pilgrims,' he said. 'What kind of pilgrimage is this, Brother? Are you pilgrims to the new East Pakistan?'

'No, we are not pilgrims to the new Pakistan,' Satu vehemently spoke out. 'Our country is being divided—taken to bits—our own people separated from us. Those who accept such prognosis are welcome to do so. We are not adherents of such eventuality, therefore, even that portion of the land that the foreigners have taken away from us is for us a place of pilgrimage; the whole of the country is! Did not Gandhiji claim that the whole country is his?'

The man laughed all over again, making an ugly screeching sound. The signal bell almost simultaneously rang out loudly. The puri-seller, however, shook his head and reassured them saying, 'There is still an hour to go for the train to leave. Have some sweets and water to drink. The train to Pakistan is going empty.'

'Do you know what it is to get knocked down (*gutto bojhen*)?' As soon as the puri-seller stopped talking, the tall dark man smiled, baring his teeth, and his East Bengal dialect became all too clear. 'Go where you must, but just don't indulge in that kind of frivolous talks there. You'll get knocked down really and truly, if you do. Gandhiji is out of his mind. He can say whatever he pleases; the papers can carry them. But you must not make such frivolous jokes. If you do, you will be treated as a lunatic.'

'Yes, Gandhiji is mad, but you are an ass!' Satu took the water jug and poured some water down his gullet. 'You are an obnoxious person; you really have a communal mind. When the entire country is singing a ditty to the unity of Hindu and Muslims, chorusing "Hindu–Muslim Bhai Bhai", you are putting the fear of God into their lives, spreading the seeds of communalism! One should hand you over to the police, man!'

The man did not laugh raucously as before, but smiled. Then ceasing to smile and giving a piercing look at the boys, he said, forcing the words through his teeth, 'I can catch hold of the three of you and finish you off in this Naihati station itself. And then send off your carcasses to Beliaghata. Don't brag overmuch—"Hindu–Muslim Bhai Bhai" indeed! The sister fuckers! *Halai koiche pungir bhai, anander sima nei*. Go, go there, and if you have eyes to see, then do take a look at the state in which the brothers of your community are.'

Satu was about to say something when Biju intervened, 'Enough, don't argue pointlessly, Satu. Gora, take the water pitcher. And yes, how much do we owe you?' turning to the puri-seller, he asked.

'I am going to get some packets of cigarettes,' Satu said, going forward to the cigarette kiosk.

'Aren't you all communists?' The man again bared his teeth and gave a laugh.

Now Gora was visibly angry. He twirled his moustache and glared at the man. 'No, we are Hindu Mahasabha followers.' Just then the bell rang loudly. Biju pulled Gora's hand and said, 'Come, let's go.'

The whistle sounded and the train was about to start. With Gora carrying the water pitcher, the three ran towards the train. They turned the handle of one of the first-class compartments. It was closed from the inside. Then the second compartment, and finally the third came ajar as soon as they turned the handle. By then, the whistle had begun to sound loudly and the train started to move. Though the compartment had one dim bulb, nothing could be clearly seen. The three friends climbed into it in a hurry. The train picked up slow speed, while the three friends gave a thorough look at the compartment, both the top and the bottom, before shutting the door. It was not clear to them if they had got into a first-class or a second-class compartment; in fact there was hardly any difference between the two in an express train. There was someone lying on the bunk below with its back towards them; in the dim light, the person lying appeared shadowy and indistinct, but covered from head to foot. There was something resembling a pillow—perhaps a suitcase with a cover—placed below the head.

Satu tried to switch on one of the lights, but it didn't come on. A fan started to rotate slowly after he pressed several buttons. But Biju's eyes dazzled as soon as he opened the bathroom door. The light inside the toilet was both powerful and bright. He kept its door ajar, letting some of its brightness penetrate the compartment. It was strange that the figure covered from head to foot in a green-coloured sheet did not even once turn to his side or give the three friends a look. They exchanged glances with each other, making a note of this.

Gora placed the water pitcher against the wall below a mirror. Satu got up and shut an open door and locked it up tightly. The three settled down on the bunk below. The train had by then gathered speed. Biju got up next and closed the two windows facing the west. One could see the scene outside from the window facing the east, rather indistinctly. There were not many days left for the night of the full moon; today was perhaps the twelfth or the thirteenth day of the lunar calendar. The sky was overcast by a thin layer of milky cloud, the moonbeam scarcely visible through it.

Satu took the cigarette packets out from his trouser pockets. He opened one, gave two cigarettes to Gora and Biju, took one himself, and lit it. He gave the matchbox to Gora after extinguishing the lit-up matchstick. Biju was smiling. The three glanced again at the head-to-toe-covered figure, as still as a corpse, and exchanged looks among themselves. They could not make any head or tail out of the situation.

'Let me go and put off the bathroom light,' Biju suggested, getting up. 'It's so bright, it's hurting the eye. It were better if we had mild lights. Besides, the moonbeam would become visible once the clouds move away.'

Biju sat down after shutting the bathroom door. They were not feeling bad sitting in near darkness with only one dim bulb lit in the compartment. Satu gave a long pull at his fag. 'I felt like beating up that darkie scoundrel,' he said. 'How dare hc call Gandhiji a madman? He's so damned communal. It is Hindus like him who cause riots.'

'And, of course, Gora must make friends with such people,' Biju said laughing, and breathed out the smoke from his nostrils. Poor Gora felt both surprised and helpless at this remark. 'Do you think I went and spoke to him on my own? He had himself come to me to make my acquaintance. He thought I was one of those who had fled Naihati and had arrived here. Then hearing us say what we did, he began to talk like that. How can you blame me for it?'

'And you became bewildered by what he had to say,' Satu's eyes were fixed at the figure lying in the opposite bunk. 'You were already frightened by the talk of the Sealdah ticket collectors. Mr Miller had the last word. I consider him to be an intelligent being. Didn't he say that there was uneasiness and provocation everywhere, but no danger? I do not claim each one of us is a Mahatma Gandhi, and we can go to Noakhali in the midst of all the rioting like he did. I liked Mr Miller's words, describing him as a great pilgrim. Where are we actually heading for? A part of our own divided country. We are going there to observe it become independent. How can I even begin to explain to that rotten man the actual meaning of Gandhi's statement, "The whole country belongs to me"? Gandhiji had not only said that; he had declared that he would like to go and live in Pakistan. What does that mean? That Pakistan has been formed out of a portion of our own country. That's all, and he still wants to go and live there. He does not want to sever his connection with that part of the country. It makes no difference to him what is called Hindustan or what Pakistan.'

Gora sounded helpless. 'Have I said I don't believe in all what you say? If I had, I would have left forthwith. But, I realize that the person is a bad one. He had arrived at Naihati a few years before partition, has relatives in these regions, and some business interests too. But to think of it, I feel that his real intention is to exploit those Hindus who have fled Naihati out of fear. Get them places to rent, or land to buy. I now get a hang of what he is about.'

'No, I am not saying anything to you, Gora.' Satu stretched himself comfortably in his seat and spread out his legs. 'I am pining away for someone.'

Biju smiled, 'I know that.'

'Who do you think it is?' Satu screwed his brows and sent a smile through his stubbled cheeks.

Biju gave him a curious glance. 'The person who is now asleep with the child in her arms.'

'You are such a dumb!' Satu pulled at his cigarette. 'The person I am pining for is perhaps listening to the radio now. I am sure the radio will be broadcasting all kinds of programmes till the wee hours of the morning—the complete play of Sachin Sengupta included.'

'I wouldn't have listened for so long,' Gora gave a rather dejected smile. 'Would have stayed as long as it is fit for a private tutor of a student. Have you forgotten that she is expecting her widowed sister-in-law today?'

'Satu, enough of all this,' Biju raised his finger and objected. 'Smoke a ciggie, then drink some water, and let us all go to sleep after a visit to the toilet,' he added.

Gora stopped in the midst of his placing a cigarette in between his lips and looked askance at the opposite bunk. His eyes were full of curiosity, 'Damn! *Shala*, can't make out whether the thing is alive or dead, be it a male or a female!'

'What can be donc now?' Satu got up. 'We'll have to call him and wake him up.'

There was a shadow of discomfiture on Biju's face, 'Really, it seems such an unnecessary trouble. I was looking forward to shutting doors and windows and having a good night's sleep. There's no possibility of that now. Why keep standing, Satu?'

'I want to go to the toilet once. Where's the train's next stoppage, can you say?' he threw the ciggie out of the window after taking a strong pull.

'Ranaghat.'

All of a sudden, hearing a deep baritone voice, the three were taken by surprise. They stared unbelievingly at the prostate figure covered from head to foot. But the figure did not move. Was the word Ranaghat uttered by the person clothed in sheet? But who else could it be? Not any one among them—the voice was unlike any of theirs.

'Where are you travelling to?' Satu asked, not knowing whether to address the phenomenon or not. He looked sheepishly at his friends.

A voice deep and baritone like the one before boomed from the figure clad from head to foot, 'Sir, I will be going to Rangpur. Where would you all be going?'

Satu looked up at Biju and Gora preparing to give a reply. Then, clearing his throat by a slight cough, he said, 'We are not yet sure. Perhaps, we'll go to Rangpur.'

The cover on top of the figure lifted and a face appeared and turned towards the three friends. A rather fair-looking face covered with silvery stubble. The hair was also silvery white, a lined forehead, and brows that had begun to take on a shade of grey, a sharp nose, rather large eyes, which were half shut. How old could he be? The boys wondered. Sixty, seventy, or eighty? One could not see his arms. They were wrapped in a sheet. Only a face smiling was visible. 'If you come to Rangpur, then be the guest of this poor self, please do. Now go to sleep comfortably shutting the doors and windows. You have no fear on my score. I am a living person, not a dacoit or a robber. We can have a chat after you wake up in the morning. But one thing, be sure not to open the door if anybody knocks at Bheramara or Ishawardi. I would have shut all the doors and windows, as soon as the train started to run at Naihati itself, had you not got in. You are all here, so I can sleep in peace. Sons, you too go to sleep.'

The face, full of silvery stubble, again got hidden behind the green sheet. He slept with his back to them as before. The three friends exchanged surprised glances, but there was not a trace of anxiety on their faces now. Rather, a note of wonder, especially in Biju's eyes. He touched his forehead with his palm. Satu and Gora smiled. The North Bengal Express chugged away, while moonlight danced down the green meadows under a clear sky.

All of a sudden, Biju was wide awake. He had been sleeping on the upper berth. Gora was below him, and Satu on the upper berth opposite. Gora and Satu were both still asleep. Biju stayed still, though no longer asleep. The train was moving very fast indeed. Had it stopped somewhere in between? He saw one of the berths below empty—no, not quite, as a suitcase with a blue cover, and a folded green sheet lay there. The light, as dim as ever, was still lit in the compartment.

Biju screwed his face. Where had the fair-faced, grey-stubbled gentleman gone? The door of the bathroom came ajar and the bright light of the bathroom fell inside the room. Biju saw the silvery stubbled, fair-faced gentleman wearing a lungi and a white panjabi. His face and his stubble all the more bright and glistening in the strong bathroom light. He carried a red *gamchha* (towel) in his hand, had a pair of albert shoes on his feet, was of middling stature, and well-built. He came out of the bathroom, gave a look around, and pulled the door shut. He sat on his seat, took out a pocket watch, and put it back after noting the time. Then he placed the towel on the handle of his seat.

His next action was to bring out a folded white skull cap from the right-hand pocket of his panjabi. He fitted the embroidered white skull cap of fine *addi* cloth onto his head, opened the suitcase, and brought out an unfolded mat, placing it on the floor. He took off his shoes and stood on the mat facing the west, raised the palms of both his hands, and brought them close to his eyes, his grey beard shaking as he sat down with folded knees. He placed his hands on either side and gave a deep bow, then straightened himself up, but repeated the movement soon again. His beard was jouncing, mouth trembling. It was clear he was uttering something, bringing his head down all over again.

Biju guessed that the man was saying his namaz. He had had an inkling the evening before that the gentleman was a Muslim, not only because of his silvery moustache and beard but because he had asked Biju and his friends to be his guests (*mehmans*), should they stop over at Rangpur. He felt as if he was hearing the morning azan ringing in his ears. Although his own house was far from the masjids, he would hear the sound of azan floating in when, during the wee hours of the morning at the end of summer, he would sit down to prepare his lessons.

The azan soon came to an end. The holy man folded his mat and placed it inside the suitcase, then taking his seat he turned to Biju who immediately shut his eyes. He opened them after a minute and, twitching his eyes, gave the man a look. The man had taken his seat next to the window, opened its shutters, and was looking outside. Biju also looked outside, but could not make out whether there was moonlight; it seemed so dark. The man soon pulled down the shutters and moved to a different place. His attention was directed at Gora now, lying on the upper berth. Then, lord knew why, drawing near the upper berth overhead, he looked up at Satu and wiped his face with the *gamchha*. His beard continued to sway as he began to mutter something to himself, noiselessly.

The train gradually slackened its speed till the wheels making a grating sound brought it to a stop. The gentleman again moved near the window and opened its shutters. The dim light outside indicated that the train had pulled up at a station. One could hear people's voices. Then one voice next to the window rang loud and clear: 'The train to Bogura from Shantahar has yet to arrive. Can you tell me, Sir, when the motor bus is scheduled to depart?'

The voice that had put the question soon moved away. One couldn't hear what the answer was. Was the station in which the train had stopped Shantahar? Biju wondered. How far was Rangpur from here? Biju had the idea that Shantahar was a big railway junction, but one could not find crowds rushing all about the place, or people shouting; nothing could be heard. The old silvery stubbled, handsome gentleman took out his pocket watch, and then, removing its cover, gave it a look. The watch had a silver chain attached to it; presumably it was made of silver too. He soon put the watch back into the pocket and moved to a different place, pulling down the window shutters. Biju could guess that he was not going to lie down any more; his beard was trembling. He was muttering something through his teeth, soundlessly. The train began to move, and sleep soon overtook Biju's eyes.

Satu was wide awake. He found a window to the east open, through which the sunlight was flooding the compartment. He saw Gora, covered from head to toe in a sheet, asleep on the opposite bunk. Biju was sleeping in the lower berth; he had made his sheet into a bundle and was using it like a pillow. He sat up. The train was speeding. He could hardly stand and was more likely to topple over when making the effort to sit or move. Nevertheless, he came near and gazed at the lower berth. The morning's sunlight had alighted on the fair face of the bearded gentleman. He was up and sitting, gazing at the scene outside. Satu moved a bit, cleared his throat and came down his berth, then went straight to the toilet, deliberately not giving the gentleman a look. The bright bathroom light was not on. He shut the door and splashed some water into his eyes. Taking out a handkerchief from his shirt pocket, he wiped his face. Mr Miller was right; he should have brought some clothes, a towel, toothpaste, and his shaving kit along. He stared at his reflection in the mirror above the basin, viewed his soft downy moustache, and made himself look neat. There was nothing he could do about his hair. He hadn't even brought a comb along with him.

He came out of the bathroom, shutting the door after him, and glanced at the gentleman. The soft, pink morning light had fallen on his face and cheeks. He was still looking ouside through the open window and appeared like some ascetic. Satu gave Biju a push, '*Ei*, Biju, get up now! It's morning.'

Biju opened his eyes, large and black, now bloodshot. He too glanced at the opposite berth to find the gentleman still sitting as before, but there was a tiffin carrier next to him. Biju hadn't seen it before. He got up now. Satu pulled at the sheet Gora had covered himself with. '*Ei*, Gora, get up,' he said. Gora stumbled out of his seat as soon as Satu called, a look of surprise and anxiety in his groggy eyes, as if he had had a bad dream. He looked up at Satu. 'What are you saying?' he asked.

'What's there to say? Get up, it's morning. Come down from the berth,' Satu rejoined.

Biju sat up. Satu opened the two windows that were shut. A moist sky, cloudless under the mild though warm sun, was visible. Gora came down. Satu and Biju both came and sat next to him, wiping their faces with water after going to the toilet. Outside, a field stretched to horizon's end, with nothing but paddy and jute growing. It was the month of Sraban, the autumn end when the *aman* rice got cultivated. The jute plants were so tall that it seemed as if a huge forest was reaching out to the sky. In places, pools of water, formed of different shapes and sizes, lay like mirrors in their midst. In places, there were bundles of rotting jute, but not a person in sight.

They saw for the first time the East Pakistan flag flying atop a big tree, nay climbing above it, so that the green colour of the flag could be distinguished from that of the tree. One-fourth of the flag was white in colour with the picture of half-moon and a five-cornered star drawn in the middle. Of course, the ensign was not that visible, as it had perhaps rained the night before. The flag was still stuck to a slender reed; no breeze blew.

'Sons, where would you be going?' the gentleman said, eyeing the three. There was a touch of smile on his stubbly face. 'Looking at you, I feel that you are Hindus, and from your talk last night, I guessed you have come out to take a look at the divided country. I had noticed you last night at Sealdah station when you had got into the compartment of the sahib. I was sitting by the window. Will you be going to Jalpaiguri?'

Satu shook his head in the negative, 'No, we will get back after taking a look at East Pakistan. Jalpaiguri is in West Bengal.'

'Yes, that's what they say,' the gentleman nodded. 'There is no earthly reason for Jalpaiguri not to be included in West Bengal. But you know nobody there. Where can you go? Do you have relatives on this side of the country?'

Satu shook his head and said, 'We know no one.'

'Then come to Rangpur, all of you,' the gentleman gave a smile. 'You will be my invited guest in this divided country. You do not have to go through any trouble. I live in Rangpur. My name is Syed Badruddin Islam. I had gone to your Calcutta. My aristocratic home is in Kareya Road, but I had actually gone to Beliaghata to see him. Our Hindu and Muslim friends in Rangpur wanted to bring him there. He said that the people of Rangpur are honest. There's peace there. I have firm belief they will be able to preserve peace in that region. You all come there.'

Satu was gazing at Badruddin's face with admiring eyes and with a smile. 'It does not behove you to address us so formally as thou (*apni*),' he said.

'You are all educated sons of respectable families, no?' A wave of quiet pleasure played around Badruddin Sahib's eyes. You have come of age now. How then can I not "thou" you? But I am really wonderstruck that you have come all the way from Calcutta to see this country. I was overhearing your talk last night. It felt as if I was listening to what my own heart says.'

Biju also had a smile of admiration on his face. 'Did you really go to Calcutta to see Gandhi?'

'Yes dear, I had gone to see him, and because I did, I could not stay back at Rangpur on the day of independence,' Badruddin Sahib shook his shoulders slowly. 'What kind of power has Allah not given to the man? Many Muslims get angry at what I say. But, tell me sons, who else but he could have saved so many Muslims in Calcutta? Which party or which leader? Who stopped all the bloodletting that had begun on August 16 the year before? Which messenger of the Prophet? What is Shaheed Suhrawardy Sahib thinking of now? Had he not seen God's laughter the year before? Till last year, my belief was—let the English go away, there will be some settlement this way or that. The English have won. We, the Hindus and the Muslims, are supposed to live happily dividing the country. But where is happiness? Peace? How long will the Mahatma live? Is the country in a good state?'

Syed Badruddin stopped and looked outside the window. Sunlight had flooded the compartment. The train was moving slowly. The three friends gazed at Syed Badruddin's face. There was a shadow of unhappiness spread over his countenance. Satu was both curious and anxious. 'Do you think the country is going through bad times?' he asked. 'You don't read Muslim epics, do you, son of the Hindus?' Badruddin said, giving a despondent smile. 'Perhaps, you are acquainted with a couple of epics and romances. Mir Mosharraf Hossain's *Sorrowful Indus* is not *Mahabharata*. You learned Hindus should read that. Koran is our religious text, our Bible. It does not matter if you haven't read it. *Mahabharata* is not a religious text, but I like reading it. I was thinking of one of its episodes late last night.'

The three friends were struck dumb with wonder. One could not guess his age looking at Badruddin Sahib's fair visage, but he had read the *Mahabharata*. How very inexperienced and unfortunate we are, Satu thought to himself. Running his right-hand fingers slowly through his silvery beard, Badruddin Sahib continued, 'If you have read it, you will be able to recall Vedavyasa telling his mother and the great grandmother of Duryadhan, Satyavati, the day Duryadhan was born, "Mother, bad times lie ahead." He did not lie. Dhritarashtra was blind; there was blindness everywhere—darkness. Brothers and nephews fought with each other over kingdom, and all of this led to the destruction of their progeny. The division of the kingdom did take place. But why was it that the brothers could not live happily ever after with their share of the kingdom? Was it jealousy? Sons, I fear to even mention the word. I think bad days are ahead of us. Yesterday, the Mahatma had observed fast. But how did he put his mind to rest? Jinnah had said that let the Muslims give him a call, he will happily go from India to Pakistan as their Governor General. What kind of thought is this for a great man like him? Lahore is up in flames; Punjab is burning. Is it only in Bangla that the icy cold waters of Meghna River flow? There is but one person who is laughing and crying simultaneously, seated all alone in a broken building in Beliaghata, and the Congress Party dancing to the tune of Mountbatten. The less said about the League, the better. Sons, forgive this jabbering old man! Maybe the devil has taken hold of me. I have a great fear that bad days are ahead. Can't you feel the earth shake below your feet? The good days came to an end the night before last....'

The express train came and stood in front of a station. It was Hili. Satu got up and opened all the windows facing the station. There wasn't much of a crowd; only some people getting up and going down. He could see the green flag fluttering atop a building outside the station. Some boys looked into their compartment, their eyes full of curiosity. Perhaps, they all had put on the new clothes they had kept aside the night before.

The three were absent-minded. All had a serious look on their face. They were thinking deeply, exchanging glances among themselves, and at times, gazing at Badruddin Sahib's face too.

Both the Hindus and the Muslims have got what they had wanted. There is no denying that that the Congress Party represented the will of the Hindus. About the League also there was no doubt; they had the interest of the Muslims foremost in their minds. Both had opted for the division of the country in exchange of freedom. That the country had to be partitioned was a matter to be rejoiced. To experience peace. Satu, Biju, and Gora had all, from day one, talked about both the happiness and sorrow it entailed, especially Satu. Even yesterday he had uttered, 'Who else is there for us but Gandhiji?' But Biju had hastened to remind him that he was a supporter of the Communist Party, one of its sympathizers. This kind of talk did not befit him. But Satu had not been pretending; he was not able to accept freedom in conjunction with the partition of the country, from the bottom of his heart. Today, one of Syed Badruddin's sayings rang like a prophecy in his ears: 'There are bad times ahead—bad times ahead.'

What kind of bad times? What was its form or shape? He had mentioned the day of the birth of Duryadhan, had talked of the prophecy of Vedavyasa. But in which sense? Would India and Pakistan wage war all anew sometime in the future?

'Parbatipur comes after this station,' Syed Badruddin took out his silver-chain-fastened pocket watch and took a look. 'We will have to get down at Parbatipur. There is a meter gauge rail track from there to Rangpur. The distance between Parbatipur and Rangpur is twenty-four miles. Sons, you will get time to finish your breakfast at Parbatipur. It will be late by the time you arrive at Rangpur.'

The train had, by that time, left the Hili station and started to move. The three friends exchanged glances amongst themselves. Satu gulped some water from the water pitcher, removing its lid. Then the two others, Biju and Gora, followed suit, taking the pitcher from his hands. It was only Satu who, looking at Badruddin Sahib, said in a humble voice, 'And you too, Sir, must have breakfast along with us.'

'But I am observing the *roja*, my sons!' a soft smile brightened up his silvery bearded face. His face was an emblem of peace, but the large eyes betrayed a deep preoccupation elsewhere. He pointed to the tiffin carrier placed on his seat, 'I have broken my fast in the early hours of the morning. I think that Eid is on the eighteenth day of the month. I think I will be able to glimpse the moon. Sunday, Monday—yes. Eid is on Monday. My three invited guests from Calcutta will stay at my place for three nights.'

The three friends laughed and looked at each other. Syed Badruddin noticed that. His whitish brows came together in a frown, but the smile on his face did not fade away. 'Will you be able to eat rice along with us, the Mussalmans? Drink water from the pitcher? If you can't, then don't come to my house, my sons! I will arrange your stay at the house of my Hindu friends.'

'Why not?' Satu felt as if someone had given him a sharp slap on his face; his lips trembled in pain. 'If we were to spend a single night in any place in Rangpur, it will be your home. Our stomachs will be filled by food and water from your hands.'

Did the eyes of Badruddin Sahib turn moist on hearing these words? But the smile was there, brightening up his silvery beard and fair face. He placed his left hand on his chest, and raised the right one. A wave of happiness covered his deep-throated voice, which rang with a sonorous twang, 'Rest in peace and happiness, my sons! When I heard you talk among yourselves last night, I felt that I was listening to my own heartfelt words. That is why I dare say, you all will be my *mehman*, my invited guests.'

'The day after tomorrow is Eid. I had been invited by some of my Muslim friends to spend the Eid at their place. But I won't be able go there this time,' Biju's face and eyes lit up with a smile.

Gora's voice came out deep and strong, 'We'll have the Eid dinner at your home this time around.'

Satu and Biju looked at each other, taken back by surprise. How could Gora make such a pronouncement all of a sudden? They hadn't discussed the matter among themselves as yet; hadn't even decided whether they would travel to Rangpur. Even if they did, there was no guarantee that they would stay back there till the day of the Eid. Biju's lips began to tremble.

Satu turned his attention to Biju in fear and respect. Badruddin clapped his hands and uttered, 'Inshallah, what you say makes me very happy, indeed!'

Gora got up and went to the toilet. Badruddin spoke in a mixed dialect. There was a large mix of Bogura, the Pabna dialect, and the language of the northern Koch Rajbanshi, the Hindu lower caste. The three friends, coming from West Bengal proper, did not have a clue about this. To them, Badruddin spoke in the dialect of East Bengal (*Bangal bhasha*). The language the man in Naihati spoke was also an East Bengal dialect. Biju was a student of Niharranjan Ray, and not of linguistics. But he knew that West Bengal was not the ancient Bengal, whereas the original primitive Bengal was today's East Bengal. Nevertheless, like the dialects in West Bengal differed from district to district, so too it was in the East. At times, people living in Dacca, Faridpur, Pabna, Bagora, and Rajshahi could not understand the language of those living in Chittagong and Noakhali. People belonging to Dacca, the middle and north Bengal, had to listen very carefully to understand the Barishal accent.

'My sons, have I made you sad with my talk?' Badruddin looked up at the boys with eager eyes. 'I have been talking about the bad days; but don't take all this to heart, sons!' He placed his left hand on his chest and touched his forehead with his right. 'I have said whatever came to my mind. Why did I? Why is there so much fear in my country?'

Biju and Satu, both nodded their head. They had stopped laughing. There was a grave concern diluting Satu's deep-throated voice. 'I do not quite understand why you are afraid about the bad times.'

Gora had just appeared from the bathroom. A cauldron of smoke, as if from a stuffy kitchen, emanated from within as soon as he opened the door—a strong cigarette smell. Biju and Satu again looked at each other and gulped; both appeared rather helpless.

Badruddin Sahib kept looking at Gora. His eyes were full of curiosity. He turned his face towards Satu and Biju. 'I won't lose my dignity if you smoke. I not only practise as an attorney, but also run a business cultivating tobacco plants. Tobacco thrives on the soil of Rangpur. If I am a part of the tobacco business, how can I fault those who smoke? If you wish to smoke, do!'

Gora's eyes had reddened from smoking rapidly in a closed bathroom. He gave a look at Satu and Biju. Biju was amused, his lips curling upwards. Satu again, looking respectfully at Badruddin Sahib, asked, 'Do you take tobacco?'

'No, my sons, but my dad did. My two sons smoke like you,' Badruddin nodded his head. 'One of them lives in Dacca, the other stays in Rajshahi. They are both older than you. You are like my grandchildren, but have come of age and smoke. I believe my grandchildren also do.'

Biju and Satu exchanged glances. Biju brought out the cigarette packet from his pocket; both looked rather ashamed and uncomfortable as they turned to Badruddin Sahib once again. He was looking out of the window to their right, gazing at the scene outside. At times, a village came to the view, floating on the surface of an ever-extending, green grainfield and, as suddenly, disappeared. What remained was an endless patch of rice and jute. And because it was the time of late autumn month of Sraban, at places, the *kash* (water lilies) flowers bloomed. But where was the Pakistan flag? One could not see the green flag with the emblem of half-moon and five-cornered star anywhere.

Biju looked askance at Satu, puckering his lips. 'Really, it is we who are stupid? The clever one among us has come smoking to his hilt. Come Satu, take one.'

'Leave all that,' Satu said, taking the cigarette. One could see that he was not in the mood for all that ribaldry; the thoughtful and distracted look in his eyes gave it away. He gave another glance at Badruddin, holding the cigarette in his hand, and lowering his voice he uttered, 'Perhaps he won't mind, but I hesitate to smoke in front of a person like him.'

Gora laughed, 'Then why not run to the toilet? It does not behove you to taunt me. The wise behave like one who has wisdom.'

'Okay. Really, you are so clever!' Biju made a face, forming his reddish lips like a pair of bows. 'And because he found you clever, he has given us permission to smoke. The smoke and smell coming from the toilet has given the game away. Never mind, I won't raise the question of anybody's age again.'

The question of age, more than anything, makes Gora see red. His nostrils get inflated, his pair of moustache turns stiff like the sword. Satu folded and his hands and solicited, 'Look Gora, one's self-esteem is something very private. Now leave all that talk.' And turning to Biju, he said, 'Stop all that, Biju. Honestly, give me the box of matches. I cannot run to the toilet after this to smoke. I will do that in front of him when I feel like it.' He lit a matchstick and held it close to Satu's face. It went out in no time, blown by the wind that accompanied the running train. Satu then struck a matchstick of his own, and lighted up his cigarette, holding his fingers as a cover against the strong breeze, but it went out again. Biju lighted his. He looked at Gora, 'Want to have one?' he asked.

'No,' Gora turned his grim face away.

Satu smoked without uttering a word. Biju was looking at him. He understood Satu so well. So did Gora. Satu was dying to talk to Badruddin Sahib. He was not enjoying the smoke. Finally, crushing it in the ashtray, he looked up at the man. Badruddin too was gazing at Satu, his habitual pleasant smile throwing radiance on his bearded face.

'Son, I have a feeling you are—'

'He's a poet,' Biju said, stubbing his cigarette in the ashtray. 'He has earned quite a reputation with a handful of poems.'

'Yes, it is likely. What's your name, son?'

'Sir, 'I'm Satyesh Chattopadhyay,' Satu pointed his finger at Biju. 'And he is Saurindra Mitra, a first class first in Ancient History, and this, Gauranga Ghosh, has a MA degree in Bengali. He's now thinking of doing a Masters in English.'

'Oh, what darling boys you all are!' A rush of joy seemed to fall all over Badruddin's fair face, large eyes, and his silvery beard. 'When I heard you talk last night, I thought to myself that all educated Hindu boys indulge in politics. Sons, do you do politics too?'

Biju smiled, 'No, we don't do politics, but we have some interest in the Communist Party. Do you work for the Muslim League?'

'No, dears, I don't work for the League,' Syed Badruddin shook his head. 'But, sons, you must know that I am a Mussalman, though I don't indulge in Hindu–Muslim political rivalry. My sons do. They are professors in colleges. My friends reprimand me; they say it is all right that you don't beat up the Hindus, but why don't you work for the League? How can I make them understand that everybody is not fit for the same thing? I am an admirer of Mahatmaji. On the other hand, my Hindu brothers also get angry with me, as Gandhiji had a quarrel with Subhash Bose, and Subhash left the Congress Party. My Hindu friends say that Gandhiji is intriguing, selfish, and wrathful. I say to myself, Allah be merciful! Who is to judge whom? Even the most pious man seeks to protect his group or his party when he does politics. But if Subhash Bose had not given up the Congress Party, how would you have got Netaji? And will you make Netaji contend with Mahatmaji? Mahatmaji no longer does politics. Netaji does what he is best at. But Mahatmaji is above all political altercations. Why don't you all understand that if he did not have compassion, Gandhiji would not have become such a great man! We have not forgotten the

Khilafat Movement, or his message of non-violence. Even today, it is he who is leading us along the new path of non-violence! Is not the message of his non-violence more powerful than the strength of the Congress Party or the Hindu people? Quaid Azam is going to Lahore as a Governor General, while Jawaharlal and Patel are busy taking over the administration of the country. And there is one person who sits inside the ghostly rubble of a Muslim building at Beliaghata to protect the lives of the Mussalmans of Calcutta. You have realized now the implications of the two-nation theory, haven't you? He never accepted this. To him, the country has not been divided. India and Pakistan are both the same to him. He is going to Noakhali again. He will be going to Bihar, and will stay as long as he wishes in Pakistan. The father of Pakistan is travelling to Lahore to care for its people, but the father figure of India is on a fast since the day before. Dears, I have a desire to go on a pilgrimage to Haj even at this old age, but I cannot do without a glimpse of the Mahatma. You all lend your support to the Communist Party, but don't be angry at what I say. I am a Muslim. I don't do politics!'

Satu was eagerly gobbling up Badruddin's words. As a matter of fact, all the three were listenening intently. Satu shook his head vigorously, 'No, we are not angry at all. Among the political parties today, it is the Communist Party that is not communal. It is still a party for the poor. But what you have said about Gandhiji is correct. He never wanted the country to be partitioned; he didn't accept the division of the country. You also know the reason why the division of the country had to be enforced. We have come to see the divided country, thinking of what Gandhiji had to say about it. We have firm belief in his ideas, but we don't understand what you mean when you say—nay repeat—there are bad days ahead—'

'Why can't you, my dear sons?' Badruddin let go his legs and sat relaxed after a long time. 'Bad times don't come unexpectedly, like the untimely rains in the month of Aswin (September). It has been coming upon us all this time till we have come to this state. The English take us to be fools, but are we really that stupid, you tell me, dears? Tell me since when the bad times have come upon us?'

Biju's eyes brightened up. 'I believe, since 1945–46, from the time of the struggle to free the prisoners of the INA Movement, the observation of Rashid Ali's martyrdom, and the days of the rebellion of the Indian Navy. Mr Atlee had declared in England about the granting of independence to the Indian subcontinent. But there were many advisors in Atlee's labour cabinet, and the drama started to unfold thence, in scene after scene in a changed landscape. I do not wish to refer to Gandhi–Jinnah, Jawaharlal, Patel, Liaquat, Suhrawardy, Nazimuddin, Wasim Ukil Hamiddul Haq, or any one of these individuals. Gandhi does not come to my mind in this context either. Because what was taking place then was a historical episode, not a plot written by the people of this country. They were merely actors in it. In this drama, the roles of Gandhiji and the Pathan leader Abdul Ghaffar Khan were vastly different, and all the other actors claim that sitting around a table like friends, they had divided the spoils.

'Ah, Saurindranath, I don't have any idea about politics. You do because, as I now realize, you are a student of history,' Syed Badruddin said and clasped his chest with both his hands. His eyes were bright and glistening. 'Satyesh,' he said. 'Your friend talks well. Nobody in this country has written the script. They have merely acted out their prescribed roles. But if you were to mention this to anyone these days, they would be mighty angry—both Hindus and

Mussalmans. Though the leaders of the League and the Congress made so much fuss over Mountbatten, and had told him such lies, his Christian soul did not hesitate to pronounce that only he and Mahatmaji did not want the division of the country. Although a few days before, the same sahib had dared tell Gandhiji, "The Congress Party is not with you, it is with me … " My god! Even so, the Mahatma's heart did not break—why? Because it was not with this or that party. His heart and soul were by then infusing the spirit of humanity to people of all castes and creeds.'

Satu's deep and quiet voice droned, 'Gandhiji had said that he wished that God had mercy on him and took his life before he saw the country get divided. He is the only person who has claimed that it were better to wage a struggle against British imperialism for ten more years than to see the country get partitioned. And even then, we must not bow to their wishes. And if the Congress Party does not agree to this proposition rather than dividing the country, let us make Jinnah the prime minister of the entire country. Vallabh Bhai Patel did not want to see his face after he made that declaration.'

'And just remember, my sons, the words of that Pathan leader, "*Hum to tobaho ho gaeye*" (we have all been but destroyed).' Syed Badruddin's large eyes seemed to turn red, but not in anger. He wanted his tears to remain dry. Badruddin continued, 'The Pathan frontier friends of Khan Abdul Ghaffar Khan all left him. Maulana Abul Kalam Azad did not utter a word. Gandhiji had repeatedly said, "I will give my life to preserve Hindu–Muslim unity. I will never give in to the partition of this country….I cannot commit suicide. Perhaps, some person will take my life. Oh dear! Had I the chance to form an alternate leadership of the All India Congress Party, this theory of partition would have been demolished. But I have failed to do that. I know I have not been able to commit suicide; perhaps someone will take my life." Satindra, you have said what is correct. All this is a great drama, but one drama has ended, and another is about to begin. It is a drama of bad days, bad days that are ahead, really bad times. Have the flames of fury got extinguished anywhere? Punjab is up in flames. In Bengal, the fire of affliction is inextinguishable. Can't you see? Gandhiji is not eternal … '

The North Bengal Express came to a standstill at Parbatipur junction.

It was the nineteenth day of August. The three friends arrived at Syedpore from Rangpur. It was a sudden decision. It was Satu who had recalled that their friend Madhusudan's elder brother Harisadhan Prasad worked in the Syedpore Railway Factory. The family of Madhusudan was from Bihar, though he had studied in the same school with Biju and Satu since his childhood. Madhusudan's father Ramprakash Prasad had a brick kiln by the side of the Ganges River, a cement and lime warehouse in the city. Ramprasad was a much-respected gentleman in the industrial region. Satu, Biju, and Gora would refer to him as 'chachaji'. His younger son Madhusudan was their friend. He was studying law in Patna, having passed his BA from Calcutta. His aim was to join politics in the future. He too was a supporter of the Communist Party, though he would laugh and utter, '*Shala*, I cannot forget that after all I am a Hindu. Can you?'

He enjoyed joking, could sing well, and would land up at their place from Patna whenever he had the chance. His parents lived in the industrial belt of the 24 Parganas, and had a huge house and business there. Thus, it was Satu who first remembered that Madhusudan's elder brother Harisadhan worked in the Syedpore Railway Factory.

Syed Badruddin kept the three friends at his house for three nights as his invited guests. His two-storey house was close by the station in the Lalbagh area. In the eyes of the three friends, Rangpur appeared like a red city. The Carmichael College building was not very far from Badruddin Sahib's house, who painted the town red for three whole days with his Hindu friends from Calcutta. He was himself a man much revered. The district board chairman, Maulana Mohammad Amin, the Muslim League President, Syed Badruddin Ahmed, the wealthy Congress leader, and distinguished people like Atul Krishna Roy, Baladhar Sinha of Sahigunj, and Sushilchandra Deb, too, came over to see his invited guests from Calcutta. It was under the leadership of such people that during a Hindu–Muslim unity meeting, a resolution for communal harmony was adopted on the first of August last year. Satu had read this piece of news in the Calcutta newspapers.

The three friends particularly noticed one thing. And that was whether it was a Hindu or a Muslim, all the gentlemen of the area regarded them with suspicion, as apart from the extreme curiosity they harboured about the three friends, there was this disbelief and a deep desire to know more about them. It was not only questionable that the three youths like them would on the eve of independence—the night before—actually leave their country all of a sudden and come away to see a divided land. It was also something not desirable. They had indicated as much through their gestures, but had not openly expressed their opinion. No Hindu invited them to his house; all of them discussed all kinds of matters, and Syed Badruddin himself spoke little.

One day Satu asked, 'I had read in the papers that you all had criticized certain Hindus on the first of August meeting, saying that they were planning to send all the wealth and moveable property to West Bengal.'

'That piece of news is correct,' a person by the name of Bimal Chandra Roy intervened. 'Such action creates more distrust and disbelief. We all belong to the Rangpur district. We want to stay back in this country. The Hindus and Muslims have lived together in the past and will do so in the future too.' Syed Badruddin had only smiled at that time, throwing off radiance all over his bearded face. And he had told Bimal Roy, 'But Bimalbabu, why did your younger brother Mukul Roy have to leave? I mean some people are sending their wealth off to West Bengal. The situation in Rangpur is so-so, but what kind of situation obtains in the distant villages, Brother? I am saying as the president of the League, why only have meetings in the cities? Go to the villages.' To that, Bimalchandra had no answer. In actual fact, he had to swallow Badruddin Sahib's rejoinder, sitting in front of the president of the League. The difference between West and East Bengal lay in this. There were riots in Calcutta, but in the industrial belts and the villages, peace obtained. It was clearly indicated by what Badruddin had to say that the situation in East Bengal villages was not that good.

None of Badruddin's two sons were able to come for Eid, either from Dacca or Rajshahi. Badruddin's wife and daughters-in-law also never appeared in front of the three friends. They talked with one of his grandsons Syed Mansur Ali, who studied in Carmichael

College, and one other who they met by chance in the first floor of the building. His granddaughter Hasina, seventeen or eighteen years old, and as yet unmarried, was however not able to suppress her curiosity about the three Hindu pilgrims from Calcutta. She would bolt and disappear fast like a deer as soon as she alighted upon them. But her restless feet would suddenly come to a halt, like a doe with quick darting looks, when she came upon Biju, all by himself, rendering him uncomfortable and helpless.

When the time came for them to leave, Atul Krishna Roy also came along with Badruddin to bid them goodbye. The hospitality Badruddin showed them was truly unparalleled. They were not likely to forget the warmth and affection of the embrace they received on Eid. Badruddin had wanted to accompany them to Parbatipur on the day of their departure, but Satu prevented him. He uttered these words when embracing them for the last time: 'Bad times are ahead, don't forget that, dears. I am full of fear when I think about it. I will possibly get killed by someone. Saurindra, you talk so much about history.'

A fence made out of bamboo lathis was overlaid with cowdung manure, a railing went around the house above like an enclosure, and a few trees surrounding it bore *chalta* (a sour fruit), *kamranga,* and *kul* (kind of berries). The roof of the two rooms were made not out of hay, but a similar kind of grass. The evening sun falling on the treetops penetrated the gaps in between the leaves. *Shyam* and *tuntuni* birds tweeted. The three friends came and stood in front of the closed front door of the wattle-fenced building. It seemed that the entire village was in slumber. The roads were wide but untarred, and the neighbouring houses did not rub against each other. In fact, there were a lot of trees separating them—a veritable paradise of green foliage. A middle-aged person wearing a shirt over a lungi, but without shoes, was accompanying the three friends. He was dark and firmly built with graying hair. Stopping in front of the door, he said, 'You said you were looking for the Bihari Hindu, Hariprasad, no? He works in the factory....This is his dwelling.'

One could guess that the man was a poor Muslim, listening to the three friends asking for the house of Hariprasad. The middle-aged man had himself volunteered to show them the place. One could hear the sound of a woman's voice giggling and laughing, ere the man ended his speech. The sound came from behind the enclosure. Hariprasad was newly married, a Bihari Kayastha in caste, but his manners were not rural. He had passed his matriculation exam, was of twenty-seven or twenty-eight of age, and had learnt to speak Bengali since he was a child. Satu always called him Harida; he did the same now.

'Harida, Harida, are you there?'

'Who is it?' the reply came from indoors.

They could hear the sound of feet coming towards the door. 'Open the door,' Satu answered back. 'See if you can recognize who all are here.'

The door of the wattled fence came apart. Harida, wearing a sleeveless banyan and a lungi, appeared. His hair was tousled, he had a thick black moustache, and was of good health, slim and tall. His eyes were large, the nose rather small. He lifted his brows in surprise and looked at Satu, Biju, and Gora for a few seconds, as if he did not know who they were. Then, suddenly looking up at Biju, full of wonder, he smiled.

'Isn't it Biju—and you—you are Satu and this—'

'Gora,' Biju added, smiling.

'Yes, yes, Gora of course, you all here? Where have you all come from? What is it all about? Come, come inside,' the man clad in lungi and shirt came to his sight as soon as he had uttered these words. 'Goodness! Is that you, Suleiman?'

Suleiman now gave a toothy smile, 'I have come to show your house to your respected guests. Now let me go,' he touched his forehead with his palm in salute.

Suleiman left as the three friends returned his salute and entered the place. A rather large courtyard was to their front, clean swept with a jute string cot placed at its centre. There was someone standing half-hidden behind the door to their right, whose colourful blue-bordered, mill-woven saree came in their view. A smooth, plump arm with mehendi marks rested on the door. The wrist was full of red glass bangles on glass or silken thread—one couldn't be sure. Although the head was covered, the face was not. One could see a portion of the fair cheek and a bit of the eyes, and one could straightaway make out that the saree was draped to the front from the left shoulder—a sign that the person was a not a Bengali. Harida, pointing the cot to them, asked them to sit down. 'There is no direct train from Calcutta here. From where have you arrived?'

'From Rangpur,' Satu laughed and said. 'Will tell you everything. Now let us have some tea, Harida!'

Harisadhan laughed and shook his head. 'Of course, you must. I am calling your Boudi.' Then, looking towards the door, he said, 'They are all Madhu's friends, who lived together in Bengal. Give them some tea.'

'Is this your living quarters?' Biju asked, looking all around the place.

Harida shook his head, 'No, it's not my quarters; it's a rented place. I don't want any quarters here. Will be relieved if I were to receive a joining letter from the Indian Railways. Here people tell you that whosoever wishes can go away to India. But, on the other hand, if they so desire, they can stay back and work in East Pakistan. They have not asked us for any written letter to that effect; I have heard that they are about to ask for one. I have written to Baba and Madhu in Patna already. I had taken up a job for the first time in Jamalpur, Bihar. Was sent here from there, that also two years ago. Did I know then that the country was going to become independent, and that we would "get a bamboo"? I mean a "stab at the back"?'

'Bamboo? You mean the partition of the country?' Gora smiled.

'What else is it?' Harida pulled at his hair in despair. 'There's tension all the time. Apart from the local Hindus, there are some from elsewhere like us—the Bengalis, Biharis, Oriyas, and Madrasis. None are in good spirits.'

'Why's that so? Is there communal tension in this place?' Satu's eyes betrayed a mix of apprehension and curiosity. Harida raised his face and looked towards the west. One could see a portion of a two-storeyed house in between the trees. He lowered his voice, 'By tension, I don't mean that there has been any big communal event here. There is no trouble inside our factory. By that, I mean there is no quarrel or dispute among the Hindu and Muslim workers in the place. But I know that some are lying in wait to be promoted to our places as soon as we leave; that is their belief. That's why they smile and tell us, "Why not go? You are from India and will, of course, get a position there straightaway. Why stay back and unnecessarily come in our way?" They laugh when they say this, as if in joke. We too join in their laughter and say, "Yes, we are about to leave." But tell me, does one feel nice to hear such things? Besides, the local Hindus are more panic-stricken than us. One or two of them have abandoned us. The Muslims don't regard this favourably. The worry is that there is a certain class of uneducated, anti-social, and communal-minded people who speak a lot of rubbish and spread lies, although all that amounts to nothing more than invoking fear amongst us. Rather, most people here are good. The educated Muslim gentlemen mix with us a lot. We talk to each other. There are even Muslims who don't want the division of the country. But this is also true that some among these educated gentlemen are to be feared. Can you imagine they refer to us as "Jimmy"?'

'Jimmy? Meaning kafirs?'

Harida gave one glance at the door of the wattled fence and said, 'Meaning Hindu; you can also say kafir … but the number of people who are like that are really few. There is lot of tension, no doubt, which is hard to overcome! But again, to say the truth, all my Muslim friends are civilized and, most, non-communal. Some are mighty angry with the Calcutta newspapers, like ours. I, of course, read only Bengali newspapers like *Anandabazar Patrika*. But I am not receiving the paper regularly like before. The man who delivers the paper says that some unknown people had forcibly taken them away. I had gone to the station to find out what had really happened. No one, neither Hindus nor Muslims, could tell me what had actually taken place. So there is some tension; but, on the whole, we are not in a bad state. Don't have to spend sleepless nights worrying, and besides, we are now spending these few days in festive spirit. Wherever you go, you'll find people congregating and confabulating in the roads, restaurants, and tea shops, as if they have completely forgotten what it is to work. We, too, are like them. But it is different with people who work in the fields and the granary because it is the time for gathering the jute plant to make it rot and separating these.' Harida stopped and, raising his voice and looking over his shoulders, asked in Hindi, 'Is the tea ready?'

Boudi's voice came streaming in from behind the door of the large room in the east, 'Yes, I am bringing it.'

'Now, tell me about yourselves,' Harida continued, bringing out his cigarette pack and a box of matches from a portion of the lungi folded round his waist. 'Are my parents okay? I know there was no trouble where they stay. I know of this from Baba's letter.'

Biju took the cigarette packet from Harida's hands and gave a smile, 'Harida, we are now grown-ups. Put away your fag and have some of our cigarettes from Calcutta, although you can also get them here. We bought them five days ago. They will last easily. I think till tomorrow.'

'Madhu, your friend smokes in front of me,' Harida laughed. 'He takes one from mine, I take one from him. So why will I not take one of yours? But your clothes are in a deplorable state, possibly not been washed for days.'

'From August 15,' Satu said laughing. 'I will wash and dry my banyan and shirt, if not the trousers today itself.'

Biju smiled, taking a cigarette out of his packet, and said, 'Harida, will you take us to a clothes store tomorrow? I would like to buy a ready-made pyjama and panjabi.'

'Yes, all that can be done,' Harida turned very enthusiastic. 'What is there to worry so much about? If necessary, I myself can supply you three boys with clothes to wear.'

Gora clapped his hands. Harida's wife had, by that time, come and stood next to their cot. Now that the veil was pulled so low, her face could not be seen. She held four cups in her right hand, and a kettle in her left. Harida tucked in a cigarette he got from Biju inside his banyan and took the cups away from his wife, not without lowering his head and giving her a wink, saying, '*Arre*, you are their Boudi. What they say in Bengali. They are not your father-in-law or elder brother-in-law that you have to pull your veil so low in front of them.'

'Hai Ram, you all are such strapping youth. Won't I feel shy?' Boudi's voice rang with a mix of rural Hindi accent from inside the veil.

Boudi had a sweet voice; she sounded as if she were both laughing and being funny. Harida roared, 'Goodness! Such worldly wisdom coming from the depths of the veil! I say, then, what's the problem in showing your face?'

The three friends laughed away. Duliaboudi also could not suppress her mirth. She stood up and turned her back towards them, and then with one swish of her hand, removed the veil off her face. Harida burst into laughter, 'Lor!' he said. 'What are thee showing off pulling away your veil with your back towards them? Hope nothing more provocative?'

Duliaboudi, almost immediately, forgetting both time and place, turned towards Harida and bestowed a hard slap on his shoulders, uttering, 'Shameless!' Hardly had she done that and giving a sharp glance at the three friends, she ran into the room laughing her wits off. The bangles around her wrist and the anklet round her feet made a symphony of a wondrous melody.

Harida poured hot tea into the cups from the kettle. His eyes and moustache were, all glinting with joy, love, and affection. 'Silly girl!' he exclaimed. 'Know this, my friends, my wife is a good soul, rather childish, and is almost ten years younger to me. She's of the same age as the poor scheduled-caste girl who works for us. You will see her tomororrow. The girl is named Gouri (fair-skinned), but actually she is jet black, with eyes large as Mother Goddess Kali, and is already married. Dulia has learnt to speak a few Bengali words from Gouri. Besides, she picks up a word or two from the Hindu–Muslim housewives who all come and congregrate here in the afternoons. They cannot follow any of Dulia's Hindi, of course, so they are making her learn Bengali.'

It was late afternoon and the sun was about to set, although the days were still long. Though it turned dark rather quickly in these regions, the day broke early as well. The call of the birds gathered in the trees made a raucous noise.

Dulia soon reappeared, her feet making a melodious sound. The veil covering her head came down to her forehead now. Her eyes were downcast, and lips gathered in a suppressed smile. She was carrying a big bamboo tray with both her hands. When she put it down on the cot, one saw that there were puffed rice and sliced onions. She gave a sidelong glance at Harida's surprised smiling face and spoke out, 'Don't you feel ashamed to offer just tea? Is this the way to welcome your young brothers?'

'I ask for your forgiveness, my dear Goddess,' Harida lifted his folded hands. 'I say, if she were not like this, would she be my wife?' He turned to the three.

Duliaboudi now raised her hand again, about to strike Harida without so much as giving the three friends a glance. He bowed his head in faked plea whence Duliaboudi resumed laughing loudly, her body shaking. 'Does the master of the house care whether there's dinner for the brothers?' she asked. 'Does he know whether they will eat handmade bread or rice? There's no fish in the house, and even if there were, I don't know how to cook it. There are aubergines and potatoes only.'

'Boudi, just lentil and handmade bread will do for us,' Satu said sipping the tea, 'and, at the most, some fried aubergines and potatoes, and a few slices of raw onions….'

'That's all!' Duliaboudi said in broken Hindi, discarding all her so-called shyness all at once. She smiled at Satu, 'Don't know what frying and all that means; will see what I can do.' Harida took out a cigarette from his banyan and declared, 'And tomorrow, I will buy fish and cook and feed you all by myself.' Boudi gave a grimace of disapproval. 'I neither know how to eat fish nor how to cook it. Come in after you've had your tea. I will turn the lights on.'

Duliaboudi was an eighteen-year-old beauty—slender-framed with firm breasts and wide hips, large black eyes, a sweet smile, in fact, more than sweet, though not a very distinguished nose. But her greatest asset was her childlike simplicity, her unabashed love for her husband.

'We don't have to worry about space,' Harida said, lighting a cigarette. 'We have two large rooms, but no beds. You'll have to sleep on the floor. But there is no dearth of bedrolls or pillows. You all have come out without a thought, I can see, as if your hearts would break if you didn't have a glimpse of this country. Though I don't think the people of this country are overly bothered about Gandhiji, they think well of Sarat Bose. Sarat Bose railed against the Congress Party for an hour and a half, on the fourth day of this month in Mymensingh, making the people here very happy. Come, let's go in. The evening has come upon us.'

The next day, after cleaning their teeth, they breakfasted on tea, bread, fried onions, and potatoes. Harida said, 'I will not go to the factory today. Although most days I go and come away, I can't put my mind to work anymore. I listen to all that people have to say, and stand near the radio to hear the news that comes through. Come home and chat with Dulia, that's all. But now, let's go to the bazaar.'

Harida came out of the house with his three friends. As they were leaving, Duliaboudi reminded them with a scolding voice, 'Come back after you've finished shopping. I beg of you to remember that there's another person left behind in the house.'

Harida shouted back, 'I am already feeling bad that I am leaving you behind, going shopping—'

The three friends, however, found a smiling Duliaboudi standing next to the door of the wattled fence as they were leaving.

Satu, Gora, and Biju came and stood in front of a large shop on their way back, after doing a round of the market. The shop was situated at the junction of two roads. Syedpore still retained a lot of the rural ambience. It had not even risen in appearance to the level of the half-rural half-urban look of Kanchrapara. But the railway quarters had many bungalows near the railway factory, which were nice and neat. There was also a motorway taking one to Dinajpur or Rangpur; cars plied as far as Bogura, all the way from Rangpur.

The large shop was a mix of grocery and stationary. Next to it in one corner was a tea shop and a tobbacco kiosk. The tea shop displayed cakes and biscuits inside glass jars. People had congregated there, drinking tea and confabulating. Some were seated outside, beneath a tree. Harida advanced near the tea shop and said, 'Come, let's have some tea.'

Biju, slipping one of his hands inside the pocket to take out a cigarette packet, asked, 'Harida, can we not ask for a bench to be placed for us outside?'

'Why not?' Harida turned to the owner of an upholstery shop, who was a twenty-four or twenty-five-year-old youth, wearing a white panjabi over a lungi. He said, 'Selim, will you get a bench placed oustside for us?'

Selim nodded in assent and then, looking at the three friends standing outside, asked, 'Who be these gentlemen, Haribabu?'

'My invited guests—*mehmans*. They have come from Calcutta,' Harida replied, gazing at the cigarette packets kept inside a glass jar within a small almirah with glass doors. Selim, in the meantime, hollered, 'Ollah, you place a bench outside, will you?'

'Give us three teas with cream, Selim, and make ten *khili* pans for us. Sweet pans with a lot of *kimam* and Caeser cigarettes—two packets,' Harida said, standing in front of the adjoining tobacco shop.

All the people seated inside and outside the shop were gazing intently at the three friends. All of them were clean-shaven—Gora's moustache was trimmed finely, though Satu's face was more stubbly. But none of them had changed their attire. They had slept at night with Harida's dhoti and lungi on. Some people sitting on a bench outside now got up and called them, 'Come and sit here, gentlemen.'

Ollah, a fifteen- or sixteen-year-old errand boy of the tea shop, had by then brought out a bench for the three friends. The three looked at each other, and went and sat on the one they were invited to. Satu's face was beaming with a smile. Welcoming the invitees, he said, 'Why don't you also sit? How can we be seated if you remain standing?'

'Sit sit, gentlemen.' A thirty-year-old man, wearing a black-checked shirt over pyjama, pulling the bench Ollah had produced near them, said, 'I can see that you speak in the Calcutta city dialect. Have you all come from there?'

Another person, wearing a blue shirt over white trousers, almost thirty years of age, with Bata sandals on his fair feet and a lit-up cigarette in his hand laughed and said, 'Can't you see they have come along with Haribabu? They must be his invited guests. Haribabu speaks Bengali, although he comes from Bihar. And you all?'

'We are Bengalis,' Biju took a cigarette from his pocket and offered. 'Do have one,' he said.

Harida had by that time come upon them. 'Arre,' he said, 'who are you offering cigarette to? Jabbarbhai? He's the son of a zemindar. He has passed his BA with Bengali Honours from Rangpur Carmichael College, has an MA from Calcutta University, and is now a lecturer in Carmichael College. Jabbarbhai, you'll provide us with fags, won't you?'

'Don't believe a word of what Haribabu says,' Jabbar replied, taking a packet of Three Castles out of his shirt pocket. 'I have nothing in the nature of landholdings. I have a teaching job at a college, that's all. Come, have a cigarette.'

Three Castles was rather a rather expensive brand, with the picture of an European castle painted on a light blue packet—not a brand the poor smoked. Harida came and sat beside Jabbar. He introduced the three friends to the two others besides Jabbar—

Osman and Hameed. The three were friends, though Osman and Hamid were less educated. Osman was an offspring of a rural rich family, while Hameed worked in a railway workshop. All the three were married. They all held cigarettes in their hands; the tea also arrived. Harida gave out an order of three extra creamy teas. Jabbar was the last person to light up his fag. 'So, tell me how was 15 August in Calcutta?'

'It was great,' Biju said, the cream came in the way of his tongue as he took a sip of the hot tea. Licking it, he continued, 'And how was 15 August here?'

Hameed was chewing his pan. Spitting on the grass next to him, he said, 'The less said about it the better, Dada. The river of joy continues to flow unabated, but there is no Pakistani flag here. Has not been since August 15.'

'No flag!' Gora was surprised. 'What kind of a thing is this! Why not?'

Jabbar inhaled deeply and then exhaled smoke. 'What else? Because the tailors not only in Syedpore but in Rajshahi, Rangpur, Dinajpur, and in other places could not imagine that there would be so many people ready to buy flags. I believe this piece of news has appeared in *Ittihad*, *Azad,* and even in your *Anandabazar Patrika*.'

'Though we had come away to this country in the North Bengal Express on August 15 night,' Satu was laughing and pulling at his cigarette.

Jabbar's eyes were wonderstruck. 'Whatever for did you abandon your country on 15 August itself?'

'All are as mad as hatter,' Harida again gave a long pull at his cigarette. 'Come to see the new look of a divided country. These three have spent three whole days in Lalbagh at Rangpur, Syed something.'

Biju, taking the cigarette out of his mouth, interjected, 'Syed Badruddin Islam is his name. We had stayed in his house. He too had travelled along with us from Calcutta in the North Bengal Express.'

'He is a mad old man,' Jabbar laughed tauntingly. 'A person like him should renounce the world; become a pir or fakir. Maybe, one day he will become that.'

The three friends again looked at each other. By their looks, one could see that they did not approve of Jabbar's sense of amusement, nor his taunting remark. They kept quiet. All of a sudden, right at that time, a hue and cry could be heard. Someone shouted, 'Oh dear, *kale khailo re, kale khailo*.'

Another gave a whistle like a piercing cry of a hawk, and even another shouted in glee.

Almost soon after was an outburst of laughter. The three friends looked up at Harida, quite befuddled. Neither Jabbar, Osman, nor Hameed—none of them had been shouting. Rather, Osman smiled, a bit embarrassed, and remarked, 'Such uncivilized lot.'

'Low and vulgar people,' Jabbar could not help laughing as he uttered these words.

In the meanwhile, the three friends, following Harida's gesture, looked towards the road to their front and saw a girl approaching, wearing a faded red ghagra (skirt) and a similarly faded indigo-coloured apparel on her body, though the light rose-coloured, unstarched muslin scarf was rather new.

Her looks became more discernible as she neared them. Rather fair-looking she was, but at this point, sunburnt like some polished old copper. A straight and pointed nose, eyes large and drawn like the goddesses, the pupils tawny coloured, and tousled black untied hair which fell on her shoulders made into one big braid. The shameless youth in her made her seem wildly provocative. She was healthy and well-built, but gave the impression of a burning flame. She walked in the rhythm of a dance, her breasts heaving according to the beat of her movements, her wide hips also moving along with it. How old was she? Eighteen or twenty-eight? Perhaps, even gods would not know, gazing at her flaming beauty and her youthful body. Would she be regarded as beautiful? There was no easy answer to that. But the eyes dazzled at one look of her. She could ignite fire into a man's bloodstream within seconds. And possibly douse him in flame. As if she were an embodiment of Venus, the goddess of love, who does not quench human desire even in her act of surrendering. Nor brings peace into the soul. Her eyes and face were deliberatively daring, her posture desperate. She was not looking at any person, although it seemed that she was throwing off all the insults and humiliating vulgar remarks directed against her with a wry smile, perhaps even encouraging them. Her left arm was covered by the scarf, and her right hand had mehendi marks on both sides and quantities of deep blue glass bangles. She went straight into the big corner shop.

But nothing, nothing could stop all the vulgar talk, the dirty jokes, and risqué remarks.

'Who—who is she?' Satu said, the cigarette in his hands almost reduced to cinders, and his voice sounding as if sunk in reverie, not merely curious.

Harida, taking his last sip of his tea, said, 'She is the girl from the Nat settlement near this place.'

'What is that—Nat settlement? A colony of bad characters?' Biju threw his cigarette and crushed it under his sandalled feet.

Jabbar's tea had in the meantime arrived. He took his cup and, giving a sip, said, 'Settlement—you can call it a housing complex or a colony—but actually it is more like a prison, a penal colony. "Nat" stands for a kind of nomadic tribe. They know all kinds of tricks that a circus party performs, magic too, even distribute amulets and indigenous medicine. Of course, nowadays they no longer do that. More likely, they steal or rob; that was why the British government had confined them to a restricted place. It is a kind of prison, though not following its strict rules. The settlement has its own superintendent officer and police guards on duty along its boundary walls.

'Why talk so much, Jabbarbhai?' Osman had just had his last drop of tea, a pan tucked into one of his protruding cheeks. Just say that it is a penal colony, although some are allowed to venture out. Like the girl you see, Moti. She is allowed to go the shops and to the market.'

Hameed broke into laughter, 'And why is Moti given the permission?'

'Oh dear, why talk about all this?' Jabbar gave a smile, a polite and a quiet one. 'The superintendent of the settlement has a glad eye for Moti. He also has a faith that she won't run away. He even allows a few others to go outside.'

Osman's lips had reddened by chewing pan. He added, 'But the superintendent has the greatest trust in Moti.'

'If you say that, then I must repeat that all the men of the entire town of Syedpore entertain a good feeling for Moti,' Hameed made a vulgar gesture, screwing the corner of his eye and giving a wink.

Jabbar again brought out a packet of Three Castles from his shirt pocket and said, smiling seriously, 'You call this good feeling? I wonder if it is not something else.'

Jabbar and Osman now laughed away loudly. Harida also joined them. Moti had come out of the shop, setting off a tumultuous wave of smutty jokes, vulgar comments, and ribaldry. The whistling was loud enough to pierce the ear drums. But a nonplussed Moti went past them, raising dust, and with posture that seemed like an erect burning flame. Satu noticed that her bare feet carried mehendi decorations, her body was full of rapture, and she herself seemed a fleeting arrow of Cupid, the god of love itself.

Harida took a ciggie from Jabbar and said, 'She has no hand from her wrists.' Satu gave a smile to Jabbar and said, 'You take that, let us now smoke one of our own.' Turning to Harida, he asked, 'Why does she not have an arm?'

'Because the people in the neighbourhood cut off her hand with a chopper when she was caught stealing. But Moti says that she was only five years old, and one of the people in the neighbourhood had, himself, stolen the goods and run away, leaving her at the mercy of the villagers who cut off her hand. But now Moti is such an adept cutpurse that many have had their pockets filched. Lord knows what would have been the fate of people had her left hand remained intact and whole.' Jabbar lit a bidi, unsuccessful in getting a cigarette from Hameed. He blew out rings of smoke now and added, 'What more would have happened? The babus and *miyan*s would have had their pockets emptied. But enough of all that talk! The brothers have come from Calcutta, let's talk of other things. The storm has blown over.'

Everybody except the three friends now roared with laughter.

Harida got up and said, 'Come along to the market with me. Can't delay any further.' He went near the tobacco shop. 'Let me pay for the lot and also fetch the betel leaf.'

'Okay, tell me one thing,' Jabbar, looking at the three friends and flicking the ash off the cigarette, asked. 'Why did the chief minister of West Bengal, Sri Prafulla Ghosh, say such things at the August 16 meeting in Calcutta?' The three friends looked at each other. Satu blew smoke and asked, 'What words do you have in mind?'

'It's something I have read in your Hindu Congress newspapers—not in *Ittihad* or *Azad*—that Prafullababu said that the divided Bengal, divided India will be one again. We know that is what we all have in our minds. A lot of untoward events have taken place. Now tell me, what do these words mean?'

Biju smiled at Jabbar's serious looks and said, 'First of all, let me tell you that we were in Rangpur on August 16. Second, no news in the so-called Hindu Congress newspapers have any value in our eyes.'

'But the papers won't print lies in Prafullababu's name, would they?' Jabbar became more thoughtful and quiet. He stopped pulling at his cigarette. 'Prafullababu was saying one thing, on the other hand, another Congress leader, Kripalani, was saying that the nation and the Congress Party have not given up their demand for undivided India. The Calcutta English papers have reported this. He, Kripalani, is of the opinion that the unity between the two states will come about for historical and political reasons. Then what happened on August 15? Was it a farce? We, the Muslims of the new nation, don't know what to make of all this talk. When

Jinnah Sahib heard about the formula for Pakistan extended by Rajagopalachari, and which Gandhiji had lent his support to, he had remarked with anger and sorrow, "What they are offering is a shadow and something to laugh at—a maimed, mutilated, and moth-eaten Pakistan." Are Prafullababu and Kripalaniji hell-bent on making that come true?'

Harida came and stood next to them with the betel leaf. He collected the shopping bag from underneath the bench. Gora smiled, blowing out smoke, but was uncomfortable. 'Jabbar Sahib, we can't give a suitable reply to all such questions. But you must know that whatever the Rajagopalachari formula that Gandhiji may have once supported, he does not want the partition of the country. He hardly belongs to the Congress Party now. He is an inhabitant of a different universe.'

'He may be Lord Buddha, Jesus Christ, or whatever he wishes. How does that matter?' Jabbar did not only sound impatient, but slightly angry as well. 'He did not want a divided country, but it has happened nevertheless, of course without rhyme or reason. The Bengali Muslims have been pushed out and held by the scruff of the neck. Such a game was played with regard to Khulna and Murshidabad. At long last, Khulna was given to East Pakistan and Murshidabad to India. Is this Radcliffe Sahib's brand of justice? We will never be able to understand how Murshidabad can belong to India. However, the country has been partitioned. So what's the use of bringing all this up now? Do they really believe that Pakistan won't last?'

Harida gave a light slap on Jabbar's shoulders. 'Jabbarbhai's head is full of maggots. These three have come to your new country. Why are you telling all this rubbish to the poor things?'

'Forgive me, Dada,' Jabbar immediately smiled and folded his palms in obeisance. 'I feel sad having to hear so much about a moth-eaten Pakistan. The Bengali Muslims are betraying their own kin. That's why I felt compelled to say a few things. I hope you won't mind.' Then, turning to Harida, he said, 'Your invited guests are also mine, Harida. Bring them along to my place this evening to have some refreshments.'

Harida nodded in assent, 'Will come between 6.30 and 7. Let's go now.'

Satu turned back to give Jabbar another look. 'Have a few questions to ask you later,' he said. All of them were up on their feet now. Jabbar was smiling amiably, 'And I'll reply to the best of my ability.'

The four trotted homewards. There was silence among them for some time. Then Harida asked in a low voice, 'What did you make of it all?' 'Bad,' Biju looked depressed. 'Was recalling what Badruddin Sahib had to say—"Bad days are ahead." Don't know what Satu wants to ask Jabbar Sahib. I don't like all this, at all.'

Satu brought out his packet of cigarettes, 'Let's leave discussing the topic at present. We have yet to hear what all Jabbar Sahib has to say in the evening. Rather, tell us more about that Nat settlement, Harida.'

'Do you want to hear about the settlement, dearie, or about the dancing girl, Moti?' Gora said jestingly, giving an amused laugh.

Satu puckered his brows at Gora. He was too angry to say anything. He blew out puffs of smoke and continued, 'What do you mean by dancing girl? They are all entertainers, aren't they? That's what I gathered after listening to them talk. "Nat" may refer to a certain bad community. That does not mean I shut my eyes when I see her. I am no ascetic or sage.'

Biju shook his head in agreement. 'Satu, you've said the correct thing. I did read a book written by a sahib once, a book on Indian food. It had a mention of the Nats.'

Harida shook his head. 'You're absolutely correct, but the girls also know how to go about as dancing girls; they are in the same profession. They dance and sing using their own lingo. You've seen Moti; the head reels watching her dance with a solo drum. But dear brothers, don't even mention this to your Boudi.'

Satu went on, 'I want to know what they do inside the settlement.' He kept gazing at Harida's face.

'They do all kinds of work,' Harida threw away the cigarette, giving it a last pull. 'They twist thread into ropes, weave mats and mattreses of all kinds and shapes, make fans out of coconut leaves, spin thread in the spinning wheel; some also know how to use the loom. The government supplies them with colourful threads and they produce handmade towels, coarse-coloured sarees and wraps, which is to say, they earn their living. They are not allowed to go outside. It is like living inside a prison. But you've heard that there are some among the men and women who are trusted enough for being allowed to go out. It's not that some don't run away, but not many do that. If caught, their feet are bound in shackles lasting for years, and are made to work harder. I have visited the settlement a couple of times.'

'Do they allow you to go in?' Satu asked in an eager voice.

Gora gave one of his sharp smiles, 'I'll go and tell Pratima about this. I really will.'

Harida laughed at Gora and continued, 'Yes, you have to just ask. The superintendent is a Hindu gentleman, Mr J.K. Mukherji. He has his quarters inside the compound. But the officer-in-charge is more of a jailor, you can say. He's a Bihari Muslim, Arif Hussein by name. The warders are a mix of Hindus and Muslims, Bengalis and Biharis—the lot—but the majority of them are Bihari Hindus. If you go to the gate and ask for permission to enter with a recommendation from either Mukherji Sahib or Hussein Sahib, you will get the permission. Didn't I say that it is both a prison and not one? It is what Jabbarbhai has described it as a settlement. A colony or a housing complex guarded by men all along its boundary walls. They produce a special kind of indigenous liquor. They are not supposed to, but who listens? The warders are bribed or they look the other way or even drink some themselves. But often a fight ensues amongst themselves and the authorities have to control the situation.'

Biju was curious. 'Why do they fight?'

'Is there any dearth of reasons to start a fight?' Harida gave a laugh. 'They fight over goods, get drunk and make a row, or run after women. Of course, in these matters, the womenfolk are one better. They have fun getting the men at loggerheads with one another. And that Moti, who you've seen, I will not be at all surprised if one day I hear that she is sleeping with a college lecturer like Jabbar. There are rumours regarding her and a few Hindu gentlemen. Both Mukherji Sahib and Hussein Sahib are looked at with suspicion about Moti on this score. Didn't you hear that that they regard her with special interest?'

Satu's curiosity rose even further. He asked, 'In which language do they speak?'

'I don't understand the language in which they speak,' Harida shook his head. 'I think it is some kind of code language. Mukherji Sahib thinks that it is a mix of Marathi and Gujarati languages. Hussein opines that it is a mix of Rajasthani and Gujarati, but when they speak with us, they use the East Bengal (*Bangal*) dialect.'

Satu, though nearing the gate of the house, could not help but ask, 'Can't we go in just once—now?'

'Why not?' Harida said, placing his hand on the door of the wattled fence of his house. 'We can go after taking our afternoon meal and resting a while.' He then gave a shout in Hindi, 'Dulia, your obedient servant Harisadhan Prasad is present.'

The musical noise produced by the anklets could be heard from inside the house compound along with the melodious voice of none other than Duliaboudi herself.

It was almost half-past three when the three friends along with Harida came to the outskirts of Syedpore. It was at times dark, and at times full of brightness, in the late autumn's expansive afternoon. Even the clouds were playing hide-and-seek with the sun. There was a mild breeze coming from the east. The Dhabala River flowed, taking a turn on one side of the town. The gate of the settlement was to their front, its boundary walls considerably lower than those found in prison compounds. A guard wearing khaki pant and half-shirt was sitting on a stool in front of the closed front gate. He had a stick in his hands. He screwed his eyes on seeing Harida with his three friends.

Harida went near and asked in Hindi, 'Is the Super in his office now?'

'No, he's at home,' the guard then gazed at Harida's face and smiling said, 'Prasadji, is that you?'

'Yes, and Hussein Sahib?' Harida laughed, shaking his frame.

'Yes. All the officers are in their workplace.' He got up and, looking at the three friends, asked in Hindi, 'Do you want to go in?'

Harida nodded his head again. 'Yes, Sir,' he said.

'Go in and talk to the respective officers at their desks.' The guard got up and opened one side of the rusty iron gate. Harida called out to the three, 'Come along.' The three friends scrambled inside the gate with Harida.

The confines of the place was quite extended. There was a large shed enclosed by a yellow-coloured wall. At places, there was wire netting, at others a metal door and a roof at the top made out of a wavy maroon-coloured metal. At the centre was a rather big and high cemented platform again enclosed by a wire-netted, fence-like a big cage! There were many people inside—men and women—busy with work. The children were playing around them, some lying on the floor. There was a guard outside the the enclosure, seated on a stool, dozing off with his head rested against the wire netting. Hardly much noise there. At places, there were rushes of green plants, some girls and boys spinning under the tree shade, but there was much *khat khat* noise coming from the big shed where the local handloom was, and the cooing of doves. Some of them looked up to gaze at Harida and the three friends, but they were pretty far away.

Harida advanced towards the right, past the big cage and a wall to arrive at an open door. He went in. The rooms inside the building had a distinct character. The walls were painted yellow, the doors and windows maroon in colour, and there was a firm brick-built roof on the top. One side had two double-storeyed houses and the other had rows of one-storey buildings.

There was a long verandah with a tin roof to the left which led to several rooms next to each other. Harida climbed upto the verandah made of cement. There was a warder sitting on a stool in front of one of the doors. Another old man was sitting outside the door, pulling at the rope of what was presumably a wall fan of a room. The man was bare-bodied, and his lungi was drawn above his knees. An East Pakistan flag was flying gloriously inside the red brick enclosure of a pebbled ground to the front.

Harida came and stood at the door. Seeing him, the warder asked in Bengali, 'Who are you looking for?'

'Is Arif Hussein Sahib in?' Harida queried.

'He is in. Want to see him?' The warder turned his head to the dirty half-curtained door.

'Yes.'

'Then go in,' the warder said, drawing the curtain aside without a fuss.

Light was streaming in from the two large open windows at the back of the room. A man was writing something, face down, sitting at a table. He had a white trouser and a white half-shirt on. He looked up as soon as the curtain was drawn, puckering his brows in curiosity. The man was hardly fifty years of age, had a fair complexion, sharp features, his hair still rather black for his age.

Harida smiled, 'Good afternoon, Hussein Sahib! Do you recognize me?'

'Who are you?' Arif Hussein's face turned serious.

Harida again gave a smile and said in Hindi, 'My name is Harisadhan Prasad. I'm from the railway workshop—'

'Of course, of course,' Arif Hussein now smiled and looked at the three friends. 'Sit down, tell me what's the problem?' The room was exceptionally large; the overhead fan was rotating, there was a wooden almirah with its doors shut and placed in a corner, and a few old chairs were placed next to the table. Harida didn't take a seat. He pointed to his three friends with a finger and said, 'They've come from Kolkata; they want to see the settlement, that's why we've come to you for permission … if … '

'Oh, that!' Arif Hussein laughed. He gave one swift push at the calling bell placed on his table with his hand. 'Who knows how East Pakistan would regard this settlement? Perhaps, if one day, I push them all inside a truck and send them to India, my job will also come to an end.' He laughed some more.

The warder sitting outside now entered the room. Hussein Sahib lifted his face, 'Satyen, you'll be knowing Prasadbabuji?'

'Sir.'

'Take him and his friends and show them around the place,' Hussein Sahib said in a commanding voice. Then, smiling and looking at Harida, he said, 'What's there to see? This is not what the place or the people are really all about. If they want, they play games at times. Some of the women and men here can really play. They teach the children how to, but their blood responds to the call from the outer world. Unless they rob or steal, there are not many who are good like them. Go and see for yourselves.'

Before leaving, Harida said in Hindi, 'But we'll not return after the tour. We''ll have to go to Jabbarbhai's house in the evening.'

'That's all right,' Hussein Sahib said, making an effort to stand up in courtesy.

The three friends saluted and left. Warder Satyen accompanied them. Walking the way, Harida glanced at the warder and asked, 'Do you come from here?'

'No Sir, my house is in Faridpore, Madaripore. My name is Satyen Naha.' The three friends were scrutinizing him. He seemed to them around forty or forty-two. He continued, 'I belong to a respectable family, but have not gone to school. I work as a guard at the settlement. Are you all Hindus?'

Harida nodded, 'Yes, all the three have come from Calcutta. They are friends of my brother.'

Satyen's yellowish eyes turned large in surprise. 'Why come to this hell leaving Calcutta?' he said.

The three friends stared at Satyen, the thin, dark, short, and rather emaciated Satyen. Satu's voice was serious, 'Why the hell?'

'What else can I say about it, Sir?' Satyen sounded very helpless now. 'I read the newspapers which the memsahib gets each day, Calcutta newspapers. Ask Prasadbabu if you don't believe me. You'll get to see and know everything if you but keep your eyes and ears open. Do you know that a special steamer goes from Naraingunj to Goalandah each day? The Hindus are running away; only the rich and the Congress leaders are flying between Calcutta and Dacca three or four times a day. All these are news in print. My elder brother and wife have fled from Faridpore along with their children. Only my old parents have stayed back. The Hindus were slaughtered wholesale in Munsigunj only a few days ago. The womenfolk, both the mothers and wives, have been cruelly molested and raped. The train to Calcutta from Kusthia are daily stopped and looted. Tell me, what more can happen?'

Satu still sounded serious. He said, 'If Gandhiji had not been in Calcutta, the Muslims too would have been killed. All kinds of atrocities—murder, arson, looting, and rape—were also taking place there. Of course, everything is going on under cover. Gandhiji will come back to Noakhali after calming the situation there.'

'What will Gandhiji do if he came to Noakhali?' Satyen sounded hopeless and plaintive. 'Is Noakhali the only place? What of Chaudanga? What fault have the Hindus committed there? Why are they too fleeing? Are you aware why the Hindus are fleeing from Syedpore as well?'

'It's all because of the partition,' Biju said.

'But whoever wanted the country to be divided, tell me?' Satyen asked in a hopeless gesture, 'I did not. There are thousands like me who didn't want this. We don't even know why and what the division of country is all about. Now the Muslims here are saying, why there should be only East Bengal, that the whole Bengal should come under East Pakistan.'

'It's all rubbish,' Satu got angry. 'Why would the Muslims talk such nonsense without rhyme or reason?'

'I too don't know why and for what reason there is such talk, dearie,' Satyen pointed to Harida. 'Why not ask him? Haven't posters claiming that all of Bengal and Punjab would be included in Pakistan been pasted all over the Syedpore bazaar? So Prasadji, am I speaking the untruth?'

Harida glanced at the three friends. Gora asked him in a stunned voice, 'We had gone to the bazaar this morning; no posters of the kind have come to our sight.'

'Yes, the posters are there,' Harida admitted. 'What to do? Not all people think alike. Satyenbabu, leave all such talk and take them around the settlement.'

Satyen sounded even more hopeless. 'Will take you there. Come,' he said. 'But because you are all Hindus, I have dared to say all this openly. We are in for very bad times, know this? Very bad. Do you think the Superintendent Sahib has any peace of mind? He comes from Dacca. The Pakistan government has occupied 280 houses for official purposes there. Most of the houses had belonged to the Hindus; among them his ancestral lodgings. Why would Officer Hussein tell me that he is afraid to go back to Bihar, his own country? I can't understand the intentions of the Bengali Muslims either.'

'Gandhiji is now in Calcutta,' Biju responded, looking at Satyen. 'The Muslims had got butchered in Bihar while Gandhiji was in Noakhali last year. Many Muslims had then come to Calcutta to escape the slaughter. Even now, the condition in Bihar is not good at all, and despite this, the West Bengal government is forcing the Biharis to return to their native state.'

Satyen smiled weakly and said, 'Look Sir, we don't understand all these things. Gandhiji had brought peace to Noakhali; he is protecting the Muslims in Calcutta now. But what you don't realize is that inspite of the country gaining independence, the situation is getting worse each day. We had wanted to be free to have peace. Now we see that everywhere there are preparations afoot for lighting up funeral pyres. Our hearts thump in fear. When we open the newspapers, we come across news of riots and arson and anarchy in Lahore, floods not receding in Chittagong, drowning the Hindus and Muslims alike, about cow and calves dying, people begging….'

Satyen came and stood in front of a maroon-coloured door on the yellowish boundary wall. The door was shut, but notes of music playing within floated out, sounds of drumbeat matching the rhythmic tinkle of anklets. And along with it, the low voice of a woman singing a song in some unknown language. Satyen pushed open the door.

Just at that time, an eleven- or twelve-year-old boy tumbled down in front of him, making a summersault in the air. He bolted at the sight of Satyen; someone sitting under a tree was beating a rhythm on the thin skin of an instrument larger than a drum. The metal bells, strung around his body, were making a melodiously echoing sound. The man had on dirty white half-pants, was bare-bodied, black as burnished copper, with matted hair, a muscular strong body without redundant flesh, and was of forty something years in age. Next to him was a twelve-year-old girl dancing, waving her arms and shaking her hips. She was was also humming a song. They did not stop at the appearance of Satyen or the other visitors. An old woman with a heavily wrinkled face and a wisp of a few white hair was sitting and spinning under the shade of a tree. She was bare-bodied, but had on an old discoloured ghagra the length of waist to her knees tucked over her hips. She looked up once at Satyen and the others. Then she shouted something in a peculiarly ugly, croaked voice, looking to her front, and almost immediately, the same young eleven-year-old boy came running from behind the trees, as if he was about to jump at Harida and the visitors. But, lo and behold, coming near, the naked, half-pant-clad boy did a summersault in the air and stood up straight on the ground after making a full circle, all this within minutes, and disappearing soon after.

'See all the fun? They have no headaches or worries, and they work when they feel like it. But if they don't work and don't produce the allotted liquor, they get paid less. Not that they are bothered about it. Come, let's go in … ' Satyen advanced towards the western part of the complex. Harida glanced at the wonderstruck faces of the three friends and smiled. 'What do you make of all this?' he asked.

'Out of this world!' Biju's voice was redolent with admiration.'I am not thinking of all the music and dancing, although that is also wonderful, but the boy seemed as if he were floating on sheer air. What a fantastic gymnast he is at this tender age!'

Satyen, clad in loose khaki half-pants and half-shirt, tucked in at the waist, rotated the small stick he held in his hand, and said, 'They are an expert in all such tricks—walking on rope tied to the poles, lads and lasses all.'

'What do you mean—boys and girls?' Gora screwed his eyes.

Harida laughed, 'They call them lads and lasses, mits and mittens—the locals.'

'Are they not allowed to show these tricks outside the settlement?' Biju was more than eager to know.

Satyen smiled, 'If that were the case, then wherefore this settlement? Games, songs, and dance are in their blood, apart from occasional filching. If convenient, they are capable of wholesale robbery. Else, why would the British government confine them to this place? They were exasperated, that is why they have locked them up here. But they keep to themselves, work when they wish, play games, sing and dance when they please, take drugs and some take marijuana. Why should I lie about this, say? We bring them whatever they want. They distill wine from their rationed rice and molasses they get as ration.'

Harida and the three friends exchanged glances. There were cells like pidgeon holes to their right; the iron doors of the cells were ajar. There were two dogs sleeping inside it, right in front of the iron door. They raised their heads at all the noise people made, and soon drooped their heads and shut their eyes. A bad smell was coming from the cells. Gora was distinctly curious, 'What are these rooms for?'

'They belong to them,' Satyen said, covering his nose. 'I lock up the rooms, pushing some males and females inside them each evening. There is no trusting them; they may run away. Besides, there are these large sheds where many stay—men, women, children, all. I lock up the gates of the shed at night. Of course, some stay in rooms without locks; they can go and come as they please and are even allowed to venture out of the settlement. There are four or five inmates who enjoy such privilege.'

Satu smiled, gazing directly at Harida. Harida looked away and at Satyen, 'I presume that one of them is Moti?'

'Yes,' Satyen smiled back. 'You must have seen Moti in the streets of Syedpore. She is what is called a sorceress. I find that even the Super Sahib treats her with respect, and so do the officers. There are three or four warders who are simply smitten by her, as if they are her slaves. And in Syedpore, she is, what can I say, a queen bee. Just see how the woman we term as loose or bad can walk fearlessly, taking wide steps with eyes staring you at the face. Moti is one such, and despite this, all the men hold her high in esteem.'

Harida disagreed and, laughing, said, 'Satyenbabu, Moti does not stare at you. Her eyes are really beautiful, and if you say it burns you to cinders, I will not contradict. You know she does not have the slightest fear of anyone.'

'That is exactly what I said. She is a sorceress, the woman knows witchcraft, although one of her hands is amputated, the Super Sahib says that a single woman can enthrall a hundred bad men; there is no better way to punish the scoundrels. There is some truth in this statement. If it hadn't been for Moti, our wives and daughters would have been in danger.'

Satyen entered a shed, taking others along with him. The looms were making a *khat khat* noise, the thread was new, and the smell of the oil in the machine entered their nose. Besides three or four women, all the weavers were male. All raised their faces and took in the sight of Harida and his three friends. There were some women on the floor feeding their babies, pulling at their teats.

They next went inside a large space enclosed by iron net. There were all kinds of things being made, from ropes out of coconut string and jute fibre to mattresses out of jute plant. The youthful maidens had sharp eyes and smiles on their lips. The young men looked strangely curious, and some were smiling, but each one of them betrayed a suspicious look and a restlessness befitting a caged bird. A question dawned in Satu's mind. He wondered what these people were seeking—freedom? Back to their no-holds-bar red state of nomadic existence?

'Why such a big cage?' Biju queried.

'There is a covering on top, as people cannot work in an open space because of the rain and the sun,' Satyen said, coming out. 'Besides, they also send some of the produce outside in exchange of cash. Can one stop all this by simply placing a guard there? There is nothing like money; goods go outside for ready cash.'

Satu came out of the wire-netted enclosure and walked towards the shade of a tree. An old man, coloured like burnished copper, was sitting leaning against it. He had barely anything on him, save a piece of cloth tied below his waist. His matted hair fell on his shoulders like the hanging roots of the massive banyan tree, but his eyes sparkled as he turned to look at Satu, who handed him a cigarette. He brought his hands together as if lighting a match, and Satu lit one bringing the flame to him, all the while pressing a cigarette between his lips. The saliva from the old man's mouth made the cigarette wet. He smiled, revealing his tobacco-stained gums. 'Looking for Moti, are you? Come to seek her out, eh?'

He spoke chaste Bengali dialect of the region. Satu did not give a reply. The old man raised his hand and pointed westward, 'There, where there are forests of *hijal* and *sheora* trees. Go there, Moti's hut is there.' Satu turned to look back; but could not see any of the others—Harida, Biju, Gora, or Satyen. Where had they gone, he wondered, although it seemed as if the old man was giving him infallible directions. He walked past a big shed lying to the north towards the west, where lay the dark green forest of *hijal* and *sheora* trees. He was discovering a strange unknown within himself. He was going to Moti, but why? He had not once thought of going to her till the old man mentioned her name. As if the old man had sunk into his vast unconsciousness and lifted the name up on the surface. He could not, nevertheless, find any justifiable reason for this.

Satu wandered in, losing himself amidst the dark green shadows of the *hijal* and *sheora* trees. He even forgot to give a pull at his cigarette. He could spy rooms made of wattles and with thatched roofs among the gaps of trees. In the distant was an open space bounded by a wall, next to a sea of willow plants.

'Can I see your face?' a voice as melodious as flute suddenly came to his ears. Satu turned around sharply. It was Moti, wearing almost the same clothes, long-faced with eyes drawn like the goddesses, full lips, slighly reddish and upturned. She did not carry a veil anymore. Her pointed breasts were visible inside a half-opened blouse; her skirt tied below her naval came up to her knees. On getting near, he could see marks of scratches, big and small, on her face, and reddish marks on the skin over her breasts where the blouse opened. Satu felt as if he could not breathe, as if the flame of fire had scalded his skin.

'Hadn't I seen you in front of Siddique's shop in the morning?' Moti said bending her neck, her voice like a playful tune. 'Jabbar, Osman, and Hameed had come to see you, no?'

Satu nodded in assent. Moti came and stood near him, the brown- and green-flecked orbs of her light brown eyes fixed on his, a slight smile playing around the corner of her lips. The playful tune was heard all over again, 'How did you come here?'

'An old man sitting under a tree sent me here,' Satu's throat was dry, his voice shallow. Moti giggled, shaking her entire frame. 'The old man sent you and you came? But you don't belong to these regions, do you? You talk differently. I know a Bihari Hindu. Have you come to stay in his house?' Satu jerked his shoulders.

'Where is your house? Is it in Calcutta?'

Satu again gave his shoulders a jerk.

'Hindu, no?'

'Yes!' A feeble sound somehow gushed out of his throat.

For a moment, Moti took in his entire appearance from head to toe, her left hand kept away from sight.

Then, within the flicker of an eye, she pushed her right hand into Satu's trouser pocket in a rather vulgar fashion. Satu's hair stood on edge; the blood in his veins went racing mad. Moti withdrew her hand from the pocket soon after. A couple of glass bangles had broken, but she held a ten-rupee note and a cigarette packet in her hand. She promptly folded the money and stuck it inside her hair, pushing the cigarette packet back into the pocket.

Her right hand and feet were adorned with mehendi. She bared her firm round breasts—the teats were marked by reddish circles, but at places there were dark scratch marks made by nails. The flute sounded all over again, 'Want to feel my milk?'

'Milk? What milk?' Satu didn't know that in this part of Bengal, milk referred to a person's teats. He clenched his teeth felt as if and tears would burst out of his eyes any minute now. He couldn't bear to glance at Moti's bare breasts, although he could hardly restrain himself from doing that. He lowered his head and nodded in assent.

Moti was about to lift her skirt. Satu looked up at Moti; tears were already rolling down his cheeks. He pitifully implored her not to. Moti let her skirt fall. There was a surprise note in her melodious voice. 'What do you want?' she asked.

'Who are you?' Satu asked in a dry shallow voice.

'I am Moti, the Nat, the dancer. What they call the dancing girl, understand? In English, they say *nomanki* (nomadic).' She pulled the blouse over her bare breasts.

English words in Moti's lips, what irony! Taken aback, Satu asked, 'Are you a Hindu or a Mussalman?'

'We are neither Muslims nor Hindus,' with a smile that was ignited by a fiery red fire, and a voice resembling the sound of lute, Moti replied. 'We worship the goddess Ma Kali and also the pir, put around the neck both the rudraksha beads as well as the prophet's image, and eat both beef and pork. I am made use of by both the Hindus as well as the Mussalmans. I am the earth—everybody wants it, everyone wants to plough it; they incur bloodbath, wanting a share of it.' Laughing away, Moti's body trembled like some darting flame.

Satu's chest heaved; he was after all the new era's promising young poet. Moti's words pierced his heart like thousand bullets, lacerating it, and cleaving it apart. He was a denizen of an independent India or Bharat. Gandhiji had welcomed it by going on a fast on the day of independence, in order to purify his soul. The three pilgrims from India have come to the newly divided country to enjoy the festivities related to the newly gained freedom. And one among them is now listening to the oft repeated saga of an age-old history from the lips of a nomadic woman. He was frightened. Moti rubbed her body against his. 'Why are you running away from me, do you despise me?'

'No,' Satu shook his head. 'To me, you are purity itself!'

'Purity?' Moti's steady lightish brown orbs penetrated into the deep of Satu's. Hardly a minute passed and she raised her left hand from behind and said, 'See, they cut off my hand when I was barely five years old.'

Satu gazed at the amputated arm. He carefully touched the place where the hand was cut off; the skin was soft and colour a bit reddish. 'Who cut off your arm?' he asked.

'Don't know, could be any one—a Muslim or a Hindu.' Her light brown orbs were transfixed on his.

Satu could barely utter a word. He whispered, 'And you are the earth?'

'Why run away?' Moti drew even closer to him.

Satu was dumbfounded. No words escaped his lips; his eyes had turned moist.

'Will you stay the night at the Bihari Hindu's house?' In her tuneful appeal, there was the hint of a secret tryst.

Satu nodded his head in assent.

'Keep the entrance door to the house open at night.' She touched his chest with the mehendi decorated palm of her right hand and said, 'Stay alert, I'll come to you.'

Moti melted away among the bluish-green shadows of the *hijal* and the *sheora* trees.

Jabbar's house was not very far from Harida's. They found him standing in the long cemented verandah of the building. Biju, Gora, and Harida had quizzed Satu intensively about his getting lost in the settlement. He had not been able to give them a satisfactory explanation, though they had noticed the change in him. Satu had not divulged anything about his coming across Moti unexpectedly and said, 'I went to the other side having lost you. It was difficult to find the main gate of such a big settlement. At last, I was able to find you, after looking all over the place.'

Warder Satyen looked at Satu rather suspiciously. Harida smiled and said, 'Rather intriguing the affair, I must say.'

'But something must have happened.' There was firmness in Biju's assertion. He looked about him sharply. 'I can lay a bet,' he added.

But Satu did not say a word.

Osman was standing next to Jabbar. A hurricane lamp was burning inside the verandah. Harida had a torchlight in his hand. Jabbar came down a step or two and welcomed them, saying, 'Come in, Saurinbabu, Satyeshbabu, Gaurangababu. Do come in....'

'You must not worry over us, Jabbarbhai.' Harida's torch threw light on the steps leading to the verandah.

The four went up following Jabbar, who now lifted the hurricane lamp and said, 'The railway workshop and the railway bungalows have electric light, but otherwise electricity has not come to this town. But do come—' He entered a room next to the large one at the front.

Osman was the last one to go in. There was a bright light kept on the table in the room Jabbar entered. It had a chimney as tall as a minar. There was a stand for lights hanging on one of the walls, and there were three other middle-aged gentlemen inside the room, and three bookshelves that could be glimpsed behind the glass door. Jabbar introduced the three friends and Harida to the inmates while asking them to take a seat. Then he turned to the others, 'He is Ramesh Bhowmik, and comes from Bikrampore Hashrai. Haribabu is familiar with him. He is the big boss of the main office at the railway workshop. And he, Arindam Saha, is the owner of the largest shop of retail garments in the market.'

'You haven't said the truth, Jabbarbhai,' the dark-skinned middle-aged Arindam Saha, clad in a *garad* silk panjabi, interrupted. 'Say it is shop number four—Syed Moniruzzman Sahib—'

'I am introducing him in a minute, I am really.' He looked at Harida and the three friends, gave a smile, and then continued, 'You've just heard his name; he is a reputed leader of the Muslim League in Dinajpur.'

'So you have learnt to refer to a leader as a leader, haven't you, Jabbar?' Syed Moniruzzman Sahib said, smiling and stroking his grey beard. He looked at the newcomers, 'I heard that you have come to see this newly divided country from Calcutta on the day of independence itself. How does it appear to you?'

'Very good,' Biju said with a humble smile. 'We like all the people we are coming across.'

Syed Moniruzzman turned to Jabbar, 'Then why did you tell me that you had exchanged some harsh words with them in the morning?'

'Would they admit that?' Jabbar laughed. 'They are after all bhadraloks from Calcutta. It was my my mistake….'

Ramesh Bhowmik shook his head, 'No, you didn't do anything wrong. Why do Prafullababu and Kripalani make such statements sitting in Calcutta? That is what is wrong.'

'Rameshbabu, are you speaking from your heart?' Syed Monirruzman laughed and gave him a glance from the corner of the eye. 'Didn't you send a wire to Prafullababu's secretary petitioning for an early transfer? And that, despite the fact that the East Pakistan government had already declared that you can go and work wherever you wish.'

At this, Rameshbabu felt disconcerted, but did not give in. He laughed, 'Just because the Government of East Bengal said this, must I leave my hearth and home and go and take refuge in the Sealdah station bringing my children along? Is that what you want, Syed Sahib? Why should I go if things are definite, I mean clear? That's why I had sent the wire. But that does not mean I cannot criticize Prafullababu's and Kripalani's statements. They are doing us immense harm by making such statements.'

'Leave all that—' Jabbar now brought a new packet of Three Castles cigarette from the pocket of his fine cotton panjabi. He glanced at Syed Moniruzzman Sahib, 'Chachaji, please excuse us. We are smoking with your permission.'

Syed Sahib placed the stick he carried in his hand on the table and said, 'Do, do smoke. You have all come of age, have grown up. Why won't you?'

Jabbar extended a cigarette to Satu and said, 'Now tell me, Satyeshbabu, you had said you had some questions to ask of me.' Satu lit a cigarette and gave a pitiful smile, 'There is nothing new in what I had to ask, Jabbar Sahib, but you may not like it. Nevertheless, was this division of the country unavoidable or inevitable?'

'What is this you are saying, Janab?' Syed Sahib burst into laughter. 'What could have been more necessary or unavoidable than this—in our country?' Satu felt even more troubled. 'Perhaps, I have not been able to state things clearly. What I meant was, did this division take place because we—you and us—wanted it? Or because someone else made it happen?'

'Oh, I understand what you want to say,' Jabbar looked at Syed Sahib and smiled benignly. 'Satyeshbabu, the ghost of the devil that is the British must be troubling your mind, I see. Now I wish to ask you one thing. Do you possess any political belief or ideal?'

Satu smiled, 'Can't say I pursue any political ideal, but I am inclined to support the Communist Party. That may be because they are working towards the amelioration of poverty. But I cannot consider myself as a genuine communist, am more or less a supporter or a sympathizer.'

'I can see that the premise of your belief is wrong,' Syed Sahib said, revealing his pair of white gleaning teeth in the midst of his long grey beard. 'Apart from Comrade Manebendra Roy, the All India Communist Party has long before accepted Pakistan's demand as the assertion of the rights of national minority. Did you not know that?'

'I know of it,' Satu shook his head. 'Also know what P.C. Joshi or Bankim Mukhopadhyay have written or said about it. But was it not possible to honour the rights of the national minority without dividing the country?'

'No, it was not,' Jabbar pulled hard at his cigarette. 'Please try to think of the problem slightly differently. Pakistan's demand was in actuality a demand for cultural autonomy in the context of national independence and, thus, very significant. Pakistan's demand is not just the demand of a communal minority—Muslims. It is the demand of all cultural minorities in independent India.'

Biju forgot to take a pull of his cigarette. 'Isn't this a rather dangerous demand?' he asked. 'Mr Jinnah is telling the Sikhs that they are not Hindus but something different. Who knows but sometime in the future, other cultural minorties might make demands for the creation of a nation similar to Pakistan.'

'Of course, they can,' Syed thumped the table with his palm loudly. Bharat does not belong only to the Hindu Congress. I am not saying that the other minorities ought to raise their voice for mere minority cultural rights. They must also raise a demand for religious rights of the minority community. Go to Calcutta and look up what Dr Sushobhon Sarkar says about this. You have an MA in Ancient History. Why must you say such things?'

There was a big smile on Biju's face, 'I say such things, Syed Sahib, because there is a sense of fear lurking in my mind. Dr Sushobhon Sarkar is also a very respected historian to me, and I happen to know him. But what you or Jabbar Sahib have just said does not only imply the right of self-assertion among the minorities. It may incite a movement based on cultural and communal identities and, perhaps, Dr Sushobhon Sarkar would not have wanted that.'

'It matters little whether he wants it or not,' Syed Sahib now spoke out with firmness. 'You have to accept the reality. Jabbar has said the right thing. The idea of a British conspiracy is twisting and turning in your head. But besides this one wrong, what else have the British committed that is not right? If they had not brought about Pakistan, then we, the ten crore people, would have eternally remained a slave to the thirty crore people. I can show you more than one instance when we, in the eyes of the Hindus, are regarded as belonging to a lower class, as less endowed, and more or less a servant. We, the Mussalmans of India, are of a different stock than the Hindus or the Mussalmans in the western hemisphere. Like them, you have perhaps not been able to accept the two-nation theory. If you had, the Hindus would have gained, not us. But yes, the British are more friendly with the Congress Party. They have cheated us, the Bengali Mussalmans. The Hindus of Calcutta are carrying on protest meetings against the inclusion of Khulna in Pakistan. Why this when Khulna is a Muslim-dominated district, tell me? Do you you expect us to be happy, surrendering the Muslim-dominated Murshidabad to India? Or, is that at all possible?'

Jabbar got up, 'Chachaji, you talk. I have to leave.' He went out of the room.

'What is there for me to talk about?' There was an expression of disappointment on his grave face. 'We Mussalmans are here in Bengal and Punjab. Nevertheless, apart from this division of territory, we have got nothing. Calcutta has been taken away from us, although it is the Britsh who have made us dance to their tune! And then the leaders of Western Pakistan, even Quaid Azam, agreed to give up Calcutta. But it was the same Quaid Azam who had earlier declared that if Calcutta were not given to East Pakistan, then what great thing had been given. It has been a total fiasco! And we had to give away Calcutta in exchange of Lahore. However, Nazimuddin Sahib has bestowed a sweet in our hands, saying that if we give up our claim to Calcutta, then besides repaying all loans, we will be given thirty-three crore rupees. And this money would go to make Dhaka another New York. All the newspapers, *Azad*, *Morning News*,

Star of India, all of them were quietened. Arre, don't you know that in East Pakistan, the districts of Mymensingh, Comilla, and the city of Dacca are Hindu majority areas? So why did these not go to India, say? But let's leave all this talk. I do not wish to calculate the market value or the book value of places like Calcutta and Lahore. But I have to tell you that this promise of thirty-three crores is a big hoax. This will be be proven soon. We will never receive any of the money.' He looked at Osman and said, 'Osmanbhai, bring me a glass of water.'

Just at this moment, Jabbar came to the room followed by a couple of attendants wearing lungi and a loose shirt. Both carried rather big brass trays; the aroma of kebabs was thrown all over the room. The attendants placed the shiny brass trays carefully on the table, and arranged several empty plates. Besides the kebabs, there were also roasted spicy chicken and vermicelli pudding. The glass tumblers were pretty, sending off fragrance of rose water, bright and sparkling.

'You all look so serious!' Jabbar said, looking worried, 'Are you feeling unhappy on hearing what Syed Chacha had to say?' Syed stroked his grey beard and laughed. 'Well, you can say that. But forgive me if I have caused you any hurt.'

'No no, why would you ask us of our forgiveness?' Satu said, smiling. 'We hold you in high respect. You have said what you believe.'

'Now, all of you take a piece of this,' Jabbar said. 'Not to fear, it is not *bara gosht*.'

'*Bara gosht*, meaning beef?' Gora gave a good laugh, 'That does not bother us. We would have consumed if had you served it. Our forefathers loved eating beef many many years ago.'

Osman began to serve the kebabs and roasted chicken. Eating became festive; only Satu seemed a bit absent-minded. He wasn't eating. After the meal came the turn for the creamy tea and the fine Benaras betel leaf with *kimam*.

'But I don't approve of your love for beef,' Syed Sahib said, running his fingers through his beard to bring some order into it. 'What is forbidden, is forbidden.'

Harida nodded and said, 'You've said the right thing.' Both Rameshbabu and Arindambabu gestured in support.

'What's up, Satyeshbabu? It seems to me that you are thoughtful. Why not be open about it?' Satu's smile could not hide his moroseness. 'Look, I am not political,' he said. 'I am a supporter of Gandhiji. The country has been divided, but to me it is not an end of everything. Today, I have come here to experience the freedom.I will return to this place again and again, always. Will you throw me out?'

'I will if that is warranted,' Syed turned grave. 'If you deign to arrive here like Rabindranath, speaking of how you would extinguish us along with "the Arya and Anarya the Shakas and the Huns on the shores of the great Indian Ocean"(*Bharat Tirtha*), then we would bid you goodbye. I do not espouse non-violence when the question is one of establishing one's identity. Rabindranath is a bigger Hindu than even the Congress Party or Hindu Mahasabha—he has no sense of the reality on the ground. Gandhiji does not believe in the two-nation theory. But you must come, Janab Satyeshbabu. You are most welcome here, but please leave all the ideas and ideals of Gandhi–Rabindranath behind you. Remember that the wounds of betrayal we have suffered have not as yet been healed.'

Satu felt as he were listening to the voices of Syed Badruddin Islam and Satyenbabu, the warder of the Nat settlement. 'Bad times ahead, there are bad times ahead.'

'We want to hold all our friends close to our hearts,' Jabbar sounded very emotional. 'We will never show any disrespect to our friends,' he said.

'Nevertheless, I recalled the prophecy made by Vedavyasa during the birth of Duryadhan. "Bad times, we are heading for very bad times."'

The midnight bell had rung a little while ago. Outside, the moonlight seemed to be mesmerizing the earth. Was it the night of the full moon? The entangled branches of trees in the deep forest had caught on some of the magic and taken on a miraculous shape. The grasshopper droned, but not the birds as the light was too dazzling for the night. The air was still and the moonlight drenched the mute earth.

Satu was leaning against the door to the wattled boundary wall. Biju and Gora were fast asleep, Harida and Boudi were in their room. Satu noticed a goddess-like figure miraculously melt into the radiance of the light of the full moon and come to surface even nearer to where he stood, and then all over again dissolve into the radiance. The next minute, he felt a touch that made his hair stand on edge; a figure clasped him close to itself. Satu, holding the figure, crossed the courtyard and went inside a room.

The light from the hurricane lamp was rather dim. A bed was made on the floor, and the mosquito net hung. Biju and Gora were fast asleep. The goddess-like figure now disrobed itself and said in a voice like the tune of a flute, 'My arm is cut, that's why you don't like me, is it?'

'You are my truth, my beauty,' Satu held up her amputated arm. 'You are the earth. Everybody wants a share of you.'

'But you don't, friend, do you?' Moti wanted to lose herself in Satu's pyjama-clad, bare torso.

Satu touched her amputated arm with his lips and sat kneeling next to her. He raised his face. 'You have given me everything. There is nothing more to give,' he said. 'Moti, I salute this earth,' and he sank next to her feet.

Moti immediately sat up without uttering a word. Her eyes were moist. 'I did not recognize you,' she said. 'I feel I want to spend my entire life with you. Who are you?'

'I am a part of you,' Satu's voice was cracking with emotion. He wiped away the tears in her eyes.

Moti laid her head on his lap and said, 'The inmates of the settlement don't shed tears, yet I am crying. Why? So many people say so many things to me. That the people of this earth are one day going to set it ablaze, and we will cook rice in that ignited fire and protect ourselves from the cold in the warmth of the flame. But, seeing you, I can't believe in all this talk. I did not know that the world contained people like you.' Moti pulled Satu's head into her firm uncovered breasts. Satu placed his lips all over again on her amputated arm. Moti now stood up, tall and erect. She was in the prime of her youth, the figure of a naked golden goddess. Her elongated eyes looked steadily with all the desire of the world into his eyes, 'Friend, do salute this ravaged broken earth. Give it a bit of love, no?'

Satu placed his lips in the space between her two brows. 'You are my eternal love. You are that image, you are correct. You have no caste, you are the earth. This broken piece of earth stands for love to me.'

Moti went on regarding Satu with an unblinking stare. Time passed; they were both without a word, without any movement. Then a tuneful sound was heard, 'Friend, put some clothes on me.'

Satu dressed her up in a skirt with his own hands and covered her body with a blouse. Moti took the ten-rupee note she had hid inside her hair bun and dashed it to the floor. Then, putting her arms around Satu, she kissed him deeply, as if it were the final giving and taking. Then, heaving a deep sigh, she left him and walked towards the door. 'Friend, girls of the settlement don't cry. They would rather kill themselves. Will you come again to this broken piece of earth?' She stood quietly against the door and looked at him.

'I will come always, forever,' Satu went near Moti. 'I will be born again and again here.' The figure that was like a bronze statue gradually faded into the darkness. Satu followed it. But that image seemed never to disappear, surfacing and dissolving over and over again in the magic of the full-moon night. It was almost like a part of the light and shadows.

Biju and Gora came and stood next to Satu. They looked with a speechless wonder at his face. Satu's gaze was far away, far exceeding the limits of seeing.

List of Names Cited

Abul Kalam Azad (1888–1958)
A leading figure in Indian freedom struggle, president of Indian National Congress, and author of *India Wins Freedom* (1958, 1988 rpt).

Debendranath Thakur (1817–1905)
Son of Dwarkanath Thakur and father of Rabindranath Tagore; secretary of British–India Association, representing Indian interest in the British Government; founder of Shantiniketan; spread Brahmoism; and was instrumental in codifying the Adi Brahmo doctrine and came to be known as 'Maharshi'.

Bishnu Dey (1909–1982)
Belongs to post-Tagorean generation of Bengali poets. With Samar Sen and Buddhadeb Bose, he marked the advent of 'New Poetry' in Bengali literature. He was deeply influenced by Marxist ideology.

Samar Sen (1916–1987)
Post-independence poet; gave up poetry for Marxist politics and journalism; editor of Marxist newspaper *Frontier*, which was banned during Emergency.

Buddhadeb Bose (1908–1974)
Major Bengali poet of the twentieth century; influential critic; and editor of *Kavita*, a flagship poetry magazine; introduced modernity in Bengali literature; was influenced by European modern poets, especially Baudelaire.

Jamini Roy (1887–1972)
Known for his artistic originality and contribution to the emergence of modern art in Bengal; introduced living folk and tribal art to the genre, especially the Kalighat Pat with bold, sweeping brush strokes.

Gary Cooper (1901–1961)
Hollywood actor known for his natural, understated style. Won Best Actor award for *High Noon*, but best remembered for the role of Roberto, the anti-fascist hero of *For Whom the Bell Tolls*, with Ingrid Bergman as the heroine.

Pramathesh Barua (1903–1951)
Actor, director, and screenplay writer of pre-independent India. Known for his legendary portrayal of Devdas, the eponymous hero of the film version of Sarat Chandra Chatterjee's novel.

Pahari Sanyal (1906–1974)
Popular actor of Bengali and Hindi films who earned fame as character-actor. Appeared in Satyajit Ray's *Aranyer Din Ratri* and *Kanchenjungha* among others.

Kananbala Devi (1916–1992)
Early singing star of Indian cinema, trained by Raichand Boral and Bishwadev Chatterjee among others. Lead actress in New Theatres productions, known for her fine performance in several films like *Mukti*, *Adhikar*, and *Vidyapati*, etc.

Dhiraj Bhattacharjee (1905–1959)
Popular actor who appeared in several Hindi and Bengali films including *Swapna-o-Samadhi*.

Sandhya Rani
A well-known actress of the 60s and 70s Bengali cinema, known for her roles in films like *Samadhan*, *Jogajog*, etc.

Paresh Bannerjee
Popular Bengali actor who appeared in *Swapna O Sadhana*.

Agradoot
Formed in 1946, a group of film technicians signing collectively as director of films—a phenomenon that was distinctive to Bengali cinema.

Charles Laughton (1899–1962)
A popular British film actor with a wide range of modern and classical roles.

Prafulla Ghosh (1891–1983)
First chief minister of West Bengal after independence.

Huseyn Shaheed Suhrawardy (1892–1963)
Bengali politician; Deputy Mayor of Calcutta (1925); served as the fifth prime minister of Pakistan (1956–57); advocated the two-nation theory; alleged role in 1946 pre-partition communal riots in Bengal; joined hands with Sarat Bose in supporting the idea of United Independent Bengal; known to have changed political stance several times.

Fazlul Huq (1873–1962)
A major political figure in British India, later in Pakistan, specially East Pakistan; elected leader of Bengal Legislative Assembly; chief minister of undivided Bengal (1937–43) and East Bengal (1954).

Khwaja Nazimuddin (1894–1964)
Founding father of Pakistan and its first Bengali leader, who became the prime minister of Pakistan at the assassination of Liaquat Ali in 1951, also the second governor general and a champion of the cause for a separate Muslim homeland.

Liaquat Ali (1895–1951)
Highly educated parliamentarian who believed in Hindu–Muslim unity, though in the Muslim League; the founder of Pakistan and its prime minister; assisted Muhammad Jinnah in campaigning for the creation of a separate state for the Muslims.

Muhammad Ali Jinnah (1876–1948)
Leader of the All India Muslim League; first governor general of Pakistan, considered the 'Father of the Nation'; rose to prominence in Indian National Congress; advocated Hindu–Muslim unity in the early years; was a party to the Lucknow Pact (1916) between the Congress and the League; resigned from the National Congress Party in 1920. At the breakdown of the idea of power-sharing by World War II (1939), began to claim a separate state for the Muslims.

Sir Cyril Radcliffe (1899–1977)
Chairman of two Boundary Commissions set up for drawing borders of two new nations viz. India and Pakistan (East & West) after the passing of Indian Independence Act by the British Parliament. Submitted the partition map in August 1947, splitting Bengal and Punjab in half in communal lines which led to people fleeing the two provinces on the discovery they were in the wrong country while the riots ensued.

Abdul Ghaffar Khan (1890–1988)
Known variously as the 'Pride of Afgans' and 'Frontier Gandhi'; was an independent Pashtun political activist and follower of Mahatma Gandhi. Founded the Khudai Khidmatgar (Servants of God) Movement, was a pacifist, and opposed Muslim League's demand for partition of India.

C. Rajagopalachari (1878–1972)
Last governor general of India before the country became a Republic (1950); opposed Quit India movement; supported British war efforts; and founded the Swatantra Party.

Acharya Kripalani (1888–1982)
President of Indian National Congress during the transfer of power in 1947; a Gandhian socialist, famous for organizing satyagrahas.

Sarat Bose (1889–1950)
President of Bengal Congress Committee and actively participated in Gandhiji's Quit India movement. Resigned from All India Congress Committee in disagreement over the acceptance of the British Cabinet

Mission's plan to partition Bengal between Hindus and Muslims; attempted to bid for an United Independent Bengal along with Suhrawardy against the Indian National Congress after independence; led the Forward Bloc Party.

Subhash Chandra Bose (**1897–1945**)
Famous as Netaji and as the founder of INA; attempted to rid India of the British with the help of Nazi Germany and Imperial Japan during World War II; was a member of the radical wing of Indian National Congress in the 20s and 30s; was ousted from the Congress Party owing to differences with Gandhiji in 1939; placed under house arrest under the British but managed to escape.

Shyamaprasad Mukherjee (**1901–1953**)
Served as a minister in Nehru's cabinet post independence; quit Indian National Congress in 1951 and founded the right-wing Bharatiya Jana Sangh, the predecessor to BJP; demanded the partition of Bengal (1946) to prevent the inclusion of its Hindu majority areas in a Muslim-dominated East Pakistan and wrote to Mountbatten (May 1947) with the demand; opposed the bid by Sarat Bose for United Independent Bengal; was greatly affected by the Noakhali riots where thousands of Hindus were massacred by the Muslims.

Durgadas Bannerjee (**1893–1943**)
Born in Calcutta, Durgadas Bannerjee was introduced to the world of films by veteran theatrical personality Shishir Bhaduri. Some of his famous films are *Bishbrikkha, Chandidas, Bidyapati,* etc.

Niharranjan Ray (**1903–1981**)
A renowned historian and polymath, who in his *History of the Bengali People* (*Bangalir Itihas*) (1949), made a revolutionary departure in writing a total history of people of region, in the nature of the French Annales School. The importance Ray gives to the physical environment foreshadows, according to Sumit Sarkar, the current interest in ecology as a determinant of the quality of life of the people.